SALT

M Curtis Allen

For Anna, the Keeper of Secrets

And Deb, the Teller of Truths

Contents

Prologue

Words matter. They can't be unsaid. Once uttered, they hang in the air, tiny vibrations, impatient to be heard. It makes you think, doesn't it? Can you ever be certain the words that leave your lips reach only the ears you intend?

Oh, my darling. Least said, soonest mended. Loose lips sink ships.

1

Wheat

'*It's all over now, Baby Blue.*'

Like drowsy flies trapped on a windowpane in the sun, the voice of Bob Dylan was the soundtrack to the afternoon. Autumn long-light softened the landscape whirring along outside. The sky was vast, daubed with cotton-ball clouds. Hot, black asphalt snaked in a shimmering ribbon towards a distant vanishing point. The sinking Mallee sunlight conjured memories of other road trips. Galahs on a barbed wire fence up Gilgandra way, flapping like rags in a breeze; sunflowers nodding heavy heads in light that had the same translucent quality. Nights when Saturn's rings were visible through a high-powered telescope. The Universe was endless then, exploding outwards through the lens.

The road raced beside the railway for miles. The harvest had come, and all that was left of the crops was spiky stubble. In fields here and there, a farmer put a flaming torch to the earth, to raze that stubble and smooth the soil once again. Smoke drifted over the land and further north, puffs of wind blew red whirls of iron-rich dust onto the road.

Prairie Humble wound the window tight and slid the vents of the little blue Morris Minor shut. Out to the right, a thin white sheet of salt crept up from the horizon. Remnants of trees jutted out of the crust, like twisted fingers, grasping for the sky. She thought of Lot's wife, turned to a pillar of salt in Gomorrah, and smiled. It was all achingly beautiful. Just her and Baby Blue, under this arc of Heaven in a hostile Drysdale landscape, all parched earth and bleached branches.

Prairie manoeuvred the wheel deftly around yet another life snuffed out on the asphalt. *You are passing another fox,* she thought grimly. There had been so much roadkill; it was nauseating. The occasional kangaroo was to be expected, but the number of dead foxes was overwhelming, and Prairie mourned them all. *'The only good fox is a dead fox,'* her grandfather used to say, but Prairie disagreed and liked them all the same. The bloated koala with stiffened paws skywards on the highway an hour out of Melbourne was particularly upsetting.

The silos of the wheatbelt dotted the land. Ahead, one loomed in the middle of the road, like a giant guarding the entrance to a citadel. But the road soon curved, and the massive cylindrical grain building slid to the left. In front of the train-tracks it sat, old and unloved. Rust covered the long, triangular storehouse. A truck idled by the railway sidings, the driver stopped, no doubt, to stretch his legs after a long haul. Pigeons flocked on the road ahead, pecking dropped grain, moving off as one great cloud at the approach of the car.

Without warning, the idling truck lumbered out onto the road and straight into the path of Baby Blue. Prairie gasped. She pounded the horn and stomped on the brakes. Baby Blue hit a patch of loose gravel and swerved. Prairie turned the wheel hard, over-corrected, and a tyre slammed into the kerb of the siding. The car came to a full stop, rocking. Prairie sat, breathing hard. She uncurled her fingers from the wheel and made those on her right hand into a fist and shook it at the truck, trundling away into the distance, oblivious to the chaos it had caused.

'You bastard!' she muttered at the retreating rear axle and turned the ignition. Baby Blue lurched forward, but it was clear she was unhappy about it. Prairie switched off the ignition and got out to survey the damage. The left front tyre had burst on the kerb. Prairie sighed. She removed her thin blue cardigan and laid it on the front seat, slamming the door shut. She stomped to the back of the car, opened the boot and was about to hoist the spare tyre out when a police car pulled onto the gravel behind her. A young officer with an impeccably groomed moustache alighted and strode towards her, tipping his cap.

'Good afternoon, Ma'am,' he said. 'Seems you've got yourself in a bit of bother.'

'Yes,' said Prairie ruefully. 'A grain truck pulled out in front of me without giving way.'

'Seems to be some skid marks here,' said the officer, looking down at the road. 'Suggests some speed may have been involved.'

Prairie was indignant. 'I was *not* speeding,' she said evenly. 'I always drive conservatively *and* to the conditions of the road. I had to jump on my brakes to take evasive action because a truck pulled out in front of me without giving way. I can assure you, Officer, the truck driver was at fault, not *I*.'

The policeman nodded in a noncommittal fashion. 'Step aside, Ma'am. I'll have this changed for you in a jiffy.' He used the back of his arm to brush Prairie aside. That piqued her ire further.

'Thank you for the offer, *Sir*,' she said, trying to smile sweetly, 'but I can assure you that I am quite adept at changing the wheel of a vehicle.'

'Quite,' said the policeman, smiling benignly and hefted the spare wheel out of the boot. He began to rummage for the jack. 'Step quite out of the way, please Ma'am. We don't want another road incident today.'

Exasperated, Prairie exhaled through her nose but said nothing. She soon indulged herself in a smirk though. 'You've put that on back to front,' she said. The officer stepped back, puzzled and blanched.

'Quite,' he said again and pulled the wheel off. Twenty minutes later, the wheel nuts were cranked tightly into place and he lowered the jack, stepping back, brushing his hands.

'*That* ought to do it,' he said, pleased with himself. Prairie smiled, with genuine gratitude this time. At least she hadn't had to get her hands dirty.

'Thank you, Officer. I appreciate it.'

'Mind how you go, Miss. Far to travel?'

'I'm not sure. I don't think so. I'm on my way to Wheatsheaf.'

'Wheatsheaf?' The officer smiled broadly. 'We're on the outskirts right now. Town's about four miles up the road. I'm the local Desk Sergeant there – well, Constable, actually. But I'm hoping to pass my Senior Constable exam in the Spring. I'm Emmanuel Timms.' He held out a grease-smeared hand, remembered his manners, wiped it on his trousers, and extended it again. Prairie smiled and shook it politely.

'Thank you again, Constable Timms. I'm Prairie Humble.' It seemed to Prairie that the handshake lingered a fraction too long. 'Well, I'd best be on my way,' she said. Constable Timms coughed slightly and dropped her hand.

'Yes, me also. Take care now.' He jammed his cap firmly onto his head and stalked back to his patrol car. Prairie slipped in behind the wheel of the sky-blue Morris Minor and turned the ignition. The engine roared to life and letting out a deep sigh of relief, Prairie gently eased Baby Blue onto the tarmac towards Wheatsheaf.

Constable Timms watched her go and delicately touched his grubby right hand to his cheek.

o o o

The main street of Wheatsheaf was wide. It was called Grain Street and was bustling for late afternoon on a Thursday. On the left, the imposing Harvest Hotel greeted travellers to the town, with its handsome bluestone facade and balcony balustrade painted bright white. Baskets of red geraniums popped against the stonework. The publican's wife stood on a ladder, watering-can in hand. A brewery truck idled out the front, and two burly men hefted barrels into the beer cellar. Across the street, a pretty young woman in a peacock blue headscarf left a café. She paused to pop on a pair of sunglasses and then sauntered down the street towards a fashion boutique.

Prairie pulled into the kerb a little ahead of the brewery truck. In her rear-view mirror, Constable Timms' patrol car appeared and passed her on its way to the little red-brick police station, half-way down Grain Street. She collected her purse from the front seat and got out, lifted her suitcase from the back seat, locked Baby Blue and went to the hotel entrance.

'Be right with you,' called the lady on the ladder, as the geraniums dripped.

The hotel lobby was dark and cool. Prairie noticed over-head fans that would doubtless spin endlessly in the Summer. Today though, logs lay neatly in the fireplace, ready to chase out the Autumn chill that arrived like an uninvited guest when the sun set.

'Now then, how can I help you?'

Prairie spun as the landlady bustled in through the door, wiping her hands on her pinafore, greeting her with a scarlet, Luna Park grin.

'I have a booking here for a few nights,' said Prairie.

The landlady looked behind her expectantly. 'Just you, is it?'

'Yes,' said Prairie. 'Just me. I'm Prairie Humble.'

'Of course,' the landlady puckered her bright red lips as if about to share a secret. 'Arthur took that booking. You're with the Exchange, aren't you?' She took a key from behind the bar and pushed a leather-bound ledger towards her guest. 'We have a lovely room for you,' she observed, as Prairie signed in neat blue cursive. 'You can step onto the balcony any time you like. We'd ask you not to smoke in the room of course – it makes the curtains ever so whiffy – but you can puff away out there to your heart's content. Lovely view of the town from up there. I'm Felice. Felice Banbury.'

Prairie followed Felice up a flight of stairs covered with thick, green shagpile and along a hall.

'Here we are. Number Four,' said Felice, waving scarlet-tipped fingers that matched her lips. 'Communal bathrooms are just down the other end. If you need more towels or milk, sing out. Nice new electric jug in there for hot water. You were lucky to get the room. We're almost fully booked this week. Some Big Wigs in from the Big Smoke. Or should I say' – she wittered, 'the

Big Salt? I do hope they'll be quiet – if there's any problems, just give us a bell, my love, and I'll send Arthur or Stanley right on up.'

'Thank you,' said Prairie, setting her case on the bed.

'We do dinner here from five-thirty until seven-thirty. Chef has done a nice bit of roast beef for the weekend and some pun'kin soup. Black Forest Gateau for dessert.' She pronounced it 'gat-ox.'

'Lovely,' said Prairie and smiled. It occurred to her that she hadn't eaten anything since breakfast but a Tosca bar.

'Well, I'll leave you be, my pet,' said Felice. 'I'm down in the bar if you need anything.' She winked a powdered blue eyelid and pulled the door to behind her.

Prairie sank down on the bed and kicked off her shoes. Exhausted, she shoved her suitcase aside, lay down on the single bed and closed her eyes, just for a moment.

When she next awoke, it was dark and the sounds of merriment in the bar drifted up the staircase. Prairie checked her watch and saw with dismay that it was twenty past seven. She yanked the hotel room door open and almost stepped in her dinner. Felice had sent up a tray covered in aluminium foil. Peeling it back, Prairie was delighted to find a meal of pun'kin soup, roast beef with potatoes and gravy and, for dessert, a generous slice of Black Forest Gatox.

2

The Exchange

The telephone exchange sat out past the northern edge of town on Telegraph Road. Like the police station, it was built of red brick with white-framed windows. Somebody had thoughtfully planted a garden around its edges. Otherwise, it was all alone in a field, the remnants of wheat almost to its boundary. The road was gravel from the highway to the little carpark in front of the door. At precisely nine o'clock, as instructed, Prairie rang the bell and stepped back. The door was opened by a rotund man, balding and red-faced.

'Yes?' he said, peering at the road behind her.

'I'm Prairie Humble, the temp?'

The red face lit up in recognition. 'Ah! Yes! Excellent! Nice to see somebody has arrived on time for work today. Come in, come in. That's the way. You can pop your coat on this rack. Come through to my office.'

The familiar humming of the exchange was a comfort. Along one wall was a bank of switchboards, three all up. It was a small exchange. Prairie listened to the steady symphony. The nimble click of the jacks, in and out. The quiet popping of the lights as they lit up along the switchboards. The whirring of the rotary dial, commanding numbers across the region. She followed the man into his office and sat on a seat facing him across the desk.

'I'm Fidel Peterson, Regional Overseer,' he said. 'How long do we have you for, Miss Humble?'

'Well, I was told the assignment was initially for a month, but I can be flexible.' There was nowhere else she needed to be.

'Excellent, excellent,' said Peterson. 'We'll start with the month then. I understand you are quite an experienced telephonist?'

'Yes, Sir,' she said, and brought her references out of her handbag. 'I passed my exam in Sixty-One, up in the High Country. I was promoted to Senior Telephonist down in East Gippsland in Sixty-Four and spent a year working as an overseer all around the region. I've done monitor work too. I enjoy the temping now – a wonderful opportunity to see the countryside.'

Peterson nodded thoughtfully. 'Come through. I'll introduce you to Miss Wellshorn. She's our Senior Telephonist – she'll show you the ropes. I would introduce you to Miss Lee, but it seems she has something more important afoot than a living to earn. Perhaps she'll grace us with her presence later.' His nostrils flared.

Olive Wellshorn had glossy black hair, cut into a severe bob. The first few strands of grey whispered at her temples. Prairie judged her to be in her mid-to-late thirties. Olive smiled pleasantly as she was introduced and patted a seat beside her.

'Mr Peterson tells us you're *'a very experienced operator'*' (she said this with a warm smile and a slight wink), 'so this'll be a doddle for you. Our code is 5546. When we answer, we say *'Wheatsheaf, number please.'* Here's a list of the codes for the region. The STD and international calls happen through that switch.' She pointed to the switchboard closest to the door. 'When you're working that second board, you have to take the long-distance board too.' Prairie nodded. *All standard procedure so far,* she thought.

Olive showed Prairie the dockets on which they were to write down each connection, so the caller could be billed appropriately. 'We slip the dockets just in here,' she said, pointing to a series of pigeonholes attached to her desk. 'And the monitor will deal with those. That's usually me, although did I hear you tell Mr Peterson you've been a monitor?'

'That's right,' Prairie nodded.

'Excellent!' Olive beamed. 'So sometimes, it will be you.' In a low voice, she said, 'I can't really trust the others.' She was just about to get to the important matter of tea breaks when the door opened and in breezed a pretty, young woman wearing a peacock-blue headscarf.

'Sorry I'm late, Mr Peterson!' she called as she peeled off her coat. It was a fabulous coat, knee length and pale blue. Prairie noted the fine fur collar. The young woman slung her handbag onto the coat stand. Olive looked at her expectantly. The girl winked back. Olive shook her head.

'Miss Lee,' Peterson thundered. 'My office *now*, please!' The girl winced and rolled her eyes.

'Coming, Mr Peterson!' she called brightly, peeling off the headscarf to reveal a glossy platinum mane and trotted into the office, her heels clicking on the tiles. Prairie noticed with envy the shiny patent stilettos, coloured a rich midnight blue.

At length, presumably having explained herself adequately to Fidel Peterson, she reappeared, with the overseer at her elbow. 'Miss Lee, this is Miss Humble. Miss Humble will be with us for the month at least. Longer perhaps, if your time keeping doesn't improve.' Miss Lee curtsied, clearly unconcerned and held out a slim hand.

'Pleased to meet you. Call me Briar.'

Prairie took her hand, noticing the long, perfectly manicured nails and the sparkling diamond on her right ring finger. 'Prairie. Likewise.'

Mr Peterson snorted and rolled his eyes. 'Prairie! Briar! Olive! It's like a bloody fruit salad in here.' Briar turned and batted her lashes, thick with mascara, at the overseer.

'And you're the cherry on the top, Mr Peterson,' she cooed. Peterson snorted again and stomped back into his office. Olive shook her head. 'What?' said Briar defensively. 'If you're not living on the edge, Olive dear, you're taking up too much room.' She blew Olive a kiss and tottered over to her switch.

'Prairies and briars aren't fruit,' said Prairie in a low voice. 'Is an olive?'

Olive thought about it for a minute. 'Well, I don't know. But it sure as hell is great in a martini.' The three women giggled.

'Night shift is going to be a hoot, Prairie Humble,' said Briar, adjusting her headset. 'Just you wait and see.'

○　○　○

The exchange in the field out of town operated twenty-four hours a day, connecting not only the locals of Wheatsheaf, but countless outlying communities lucky enough to be within repeating distance of the telegraph line that marched like a dutiful column of soldiers, all the way to Golga.

Fidel Peterson had five exchanges under his watch: Golga up north, Blackwatch in the east, Silky Hills down south and Dumbogan out west. Wheatsheaf was bang in the centre of things, and it was his least favourite out-post. He was always happy to see it receding in his rear-view mirror, as now, dust from the gravel drive swirling in his wake. Briar Lee was mouthy and disrespectful. He'd had cause to terminate her many times, but each time, fate seemed to intervene and keep her at her post. With every passing month, he thought – *hoped!* – she would breeze in, announcing her betrothal to some poor fool, and hand in her resignation. Unhappily, it hadn't eventuated so far.

Olive Wellshorn was capable and efficient, he reflected. He was mildly intimidated by her but would never admit it. He regretted asking her out for a drink some years back, only to be rejected. He rarely allowed himself to dwell on this embarrassing moment, and as long as she stayed single, he felt they were somewhat even. And so, the seasons rolled on, one harvest after another, and Fidel Peterson, Regional Overseer of the Postmaster General, counted his blessings that he only had to land in Wheatsheaf one week in every five, as long as the lines were up.

There were five rotating shifts of six hours and one of eight hours over a twenty-four-hour period, always with two operators starting and ending at staggered intervals, except for the night-shift. There were six operators on the day shifts, meaning one would always have a complete shift off every six days. The 'grave-yard shift,' six o'clock until midnight was dreaded, especially on a weekend, because it left little time to take in a picture show, dance at the Rex, or a favoured drink at the Harvest Hotel.

Worst of all was the 'crypt shift' – ten o'clock at night until six in the morning. Nobody wanted to face an eight-hour stint through the darkness ending only when the fresh-faced 'morning crew' arrived to take over. A bed in the back served as an emergency refuge for those in need of a nap before the drive home. The 'crypt shift' was the realm of the 'Night Boys.' The isolated exchange in the field of wheat was no place for a lady of the PMG.

As soon as the dust from Peterson's black Hillman had settled, Olive turned to Briar Lee. 'Another new coat?'

'Why not?' Briar pouted. 'It's Winter.'

'It's Autumn,' Olive replied.

'Well, it certainly is chilly in here, Olive dear!' A light lit up on Briar's switchboard. She answered with 'Wheatsheaf. Number please?' and then 'Hold the line please,' as she inserted a jack to connect the call. She checked the time and scribbled on a docket. Olive shook her head and pulled out the roster.

'We rotate,' she said to Prairie. 'Like this. You've been sent to take over Patty's shift. Patty would have been on this shift here today.' She pointed to the midday to six o'clock slot. 'You do three hours with Briar, twelve to three, and then three with Mabel Wattage – three to six. Briar can introduce you to Mabel when they change over. This shift here' (she pointed to the 'crypt shift'), 'we girls never do. The Night Boys do these shifts.'

Prairie nodded. 'I think it's the same across the entire PMG.'

'Of course!' said Olive. 'You're welcome to sit in on a few of my calls now if you like. Or you can go about your day and come back at about a quarter to twelve to relieve me?'

Prairie looked at her watch. It was now a quarter to ten. She decided it wasn't worth going back into town when she could stay and acquaint herself with the girls she was to work with for the next four weeks. 'I'll stay,' she said.

Olive smiled and stood up. 'Coffee?'

'Yes please! White with one.' The switchboard lit up. Briar was on another call. 'I'll take it,' said Prairie and donned Olive's headset. 'Wheatsheaf. Number please.'

O O O

3

The Harvest Hotel

To the good folk of Wheatsheaf at a quarter past nine on a Saturday night, the Harvest Hotel might as well have been the centre of the Universe. The infamous 'six o'clock swill' had ended two years ago, much to the delight of the town and now, the honey-hued light spilled through the window casements into amber puddles on the pavement outside. Pulling up in the dark, the warmth beckoned, and Prairie couldn't wait to be inside. She pushed open the door and was wrapped in a waft of tobacco and spilled beer; assailed by the jabber of local farmers, all trying to be heard over one another.

'I didn't get half the crop in I was expecting from the far field,' said one, holding counsel at the bar. 'If the rains don't come this Winter, I'm not sure what we'll do.' Those around him nodded and murmured. 'Been bad since Sixty-Five,' said another.

Prairie's second shift had been uneventful enough. She had relieved Olive at precisely three o'clock in the afternoon, and had worked alongside Briar from the start of her shift until Briar's departure at six o'clock that evening, when Mabel Wattage arrived. Prairie left at nine, knowing Mabel would only be alone for an hour until Tom Rizzoli arrived at ten for his 'crypt shift.' Looking around the crowded hotel, she spied Olive and Briar at a table in the corner with two other girls. Olive waved her over. Prairie waved back and pointed to the bar.

'A glass of Chablis please, Felice,' she said.

'How was your shift today, Lamb?' Felice struggled with the cork from a new bottle. 'Christ, Stanley,' she said. 'Can you work the screw-thingy?' Felice's son rolled his eyes but said nothing as he took the bottle from her.

'It was good,' said Prairie. 'Quiet. For a Saturday evening, very quiet. I was surprised. I meant to ask – do you think I could rent my room for the month? Mr Peterson wants me for at least that long, and talking to Briar today, it might be a better option than me trying to find a room somewhere in town.'

Felice was flattered. She clutched her hand to her chest and for a moment looked as though she might burst into tears. 'Oh Lamb!' she said. 'I'd *love* that!' Stan Banbury came back with the glass of Chablis. 'Stanley,' Felice said, 'Wonderful news. Prairie's going to be with us for a whole *month!* Who knows? She might even stay for good!'

Stan blushed and set the drink on the bar. 'Here you go,' he mumbled and moved off to wipe up a puddle of beer. Prairie smiled.

'Oh, we'll have the most marvellous lock-ins, Lamb! You wait and see,' said Felice, patting her arm. 'Arthur! Arthur! Prairie's staying a month!' she yelled, over the din.

Prairie took her drink over to the small table in the corner.

'Prairie,' said Olive, 'This is Paula McInerney, from the Post Office, and this is Cindy Schubele. Cindy teaches at the school.'

'How do you do?' said Prairie, shaking hands with each in turn. Briar took a drag from a cigarette and blew smoke rings across the table.

'Gorgeous ring,' said Paula. 'Where did you get that?'

'Golga,' Briar replied, proffering her right hand. 'Went up there on my day off last week. Some magnificent bargains – fair shopped until I dropped. It's a bigger carat than the one I got from Evans.'

Paula turned the diamond-encrusted finger this way and that and said enviously, 'I think the Postmaster General forgot me during his last wage rise.'

'I'm just good at saving.' Briar retracted her hand.

'Who are those three men over there, at the far end of the bar?' asked Cindy. They had clearly been watching the girls. One raised his beer in greeting. Prairie raised her glass in return. Paula gasped and blushed.

'If none of you recognise them,' Prairie mused, 'then they might be the *Big Salties* Felice told me about yesterday.'

'The one in the blue shirt is *gorgeous*,' Paula murmured. Olive and Cindy looked over. Cindy shrugged, 'I guess.'

'What did Felice mean by *Big Salties*?' asked Prairie, sipping her wine.

'Blush Salt Works,' said Briar, nursing a glass of Spumante. 'It's about the only thing this area has going for it – apart from wheat. You grow up here and you either become a farmer or a salt-miner.'

'Or you leave,' said Cindy.

'Or you stay and work for the Postmaster General until you die at your desk,' said Paula taciturnly, and the girls erupted into laughter. That caused the men at the bar to look over. Prairie caught Blue Shirt's eye, and he smiled, showing a mouthful of beautiful, white teeth. Prairie turned back to the table. She could suddenly feel the roots of her hair.

'Talk about Blush,' said Briar, smirking.

At a quarter to ten, a moustachioed policeman entered the bar to perform his nightly sweep. He felt it his responsibility to usher his flock calmly from the hotel at closing time and to help Arthur and Stan eject any of the rowdy or troublesome ones. Prairie recognised him immediately.

Felice rang the bell. 'Drink up! Constabulary is here,' she hollered. The girls drained their glasses and bid each other good night. Prairie stood to make her way upstairs, eager to avoid another confrontation with the police officer, but Felice called her over to the bar. 'We're going to do a lock-in for the Salties if you want to stay for another, love?' she whispered. 'You hardly got much of a Saturday night.'

'Thank you,' said Prairie, and was about to decline, when Constable Timms accosted her.

'Excuse me, Miss Humble,' he said, 'But this here gentleman has something to say to you.' A burley truck-driver stood there swaying slightly, twisting a cap in his hand. 'Well, go on Sam. You could have caused a dreadful accident.'

'Sorry, Miss,' said Sam. He looked at the constable. 'What for again?'

Timms sighed with exasperation. 'Yesterday afternoon, Sam. You pulled out from the silo haul road and failed to give way. Miss Humble was approaching on the highway and was forced to slam on her brakes. She skidded and burst her tyre. I had to change it.'

Prairie was about to interject and point out that she was quite willing to change it herself, but Sam looked abashed and stared down at his feet.

'I'm so sorry, Miss. I didn't see you.'

'That's because you didn't look!' chided Timms.

'No harm done, Sam,' said Prairie feeling the burley driver's embarrassment. She held out her hand. 'It's nice to meet you under better circumstances.' Sam stifled a belch and clumsily shook it. Timms tutted in disgust.

'I hope you've left that truck at home, Sam Swallow,' he lectured, ushering the driver out into the street. 'I don't want my colleagues further up the road scraping you up off it!'

Prairie stifled a giggle. She turned to tell Felice she'd see her in the morning, but Blue Shirt was suddenly behind her.

'Excuse me,' he said.

'Yes?' said Prairie, feeling herself start to blush again.

'Oh, I'd just like to get to the bar,' he said and pointed behind her.

'Oh!' Prairie felt foolish. 'Of course. I'm sorry. Good night, Felice!' she called and hurried up the stairs to Room Four without looking back. She kicked off her shoes and toyed with the idea of taking a soak in the communal bath but decided against it. Instead, she pulled out her sketchpad and began to outline the silos rising from the bend in the road to Wheatsheaf. She closed her eyes and tried to remember their shape. She saw Sam Swallow's bright red truck with the golden sheaf of wheat emblazoned on the door. It was nearing eleven when she finished, but she was wide awake.

She rummaged through her purse looking for the cigarette Briar had handed her down in the bar. Prairie did not often smoke, but she wanted an excuse to step out onto the balcony and survey the town from above.

A chilly breeze brushed her face as she pushed open the balcony door. It was a refreshing antidote to the hot, stale air of the bar. Prairie leaned against the balustrade and struck a match. She watched it flare, smelled the acrid tang of sulphur and held it to the tip of the cigarette. She inhaled and, through pursed lips, pushed a stream of blue smoke out into the cold night, gazing out over sleeping Wheatsheaf. Aside from the yellow light from the pub windows illuminating the road below, and a distant lamp by the police station, the street was dark. And apart from a few lights from bare windows, Wheatsheaf was surrounded by darkened field. In Spring and Summer, crops would blanket those fields and rustle with a soft, golden susurrus. But for now, the blackened earth was still. She stared ahead into the canopy of stars and was about to look for the Southern Cross when a voice to her right startled her.

'The stars are low tonight.' Prairie saw the glow of a lit cigarette in a shadowy corner. Blue Shirt stood leaning against the wall, also smoking and admiring the view. 'I didn't mean to startle you,' he added, softly.

Prairie laughed – a bit too nervously, she thought. 'I didn't realise anyone else was up here. I thought you were all down in the bar.'

He approached her. 'I'm not much of a drinker,' he said. 'Gil Sanders.' He held out his hand.

Prairie hurriedly stuffed her cigarette between the fingers of her left hand and shook his. 'Prairie Humble.' His hand was large and warm around hers.

'Prairie. That's a beautiful name. I like prairies.' Prairie looked at him askance and he laughed. 'I'm a geologist. I find something to like about all landscapes.'

'Oh!' said Prairie, relaxing. 'At least you don't think I belong in a fruit salad.' Gil looked at her quizzically and she laughed. 'Never mind. I thought you were a Saltie?'

Now it was Gil's turn to laugh. 'A what?'

'It's what they call the employees of the salt works down the road. Apparently,' she added. 'I had no idea there was a salt works down the road until about two hours ago. Felice told me there were some *'Big Wigs from the Big Salt'* staying here, but I had no idea what she meant.'

Gil nodded. 'She's right – Blush Salt Works is about seven miles down the road from here. I'm not sure I'd describe us as *'Big Wigs'* though. At least I'm not. I'm just a geologist with the firm. The other two are accountants. Probably here to make sure my expenses don't run out of control.' He laughed again and Prairie caught a glimpse of his perfect white teeth.

'What's a salt works doing in the middle of a wheatfield?' she asked, suddenly interested, although she wished she'd had the presence of mind to put her coat on before coming out into the night.

'It's not so unusual,' he said, leaning on the balustrade, gazing out into the inky void. 'Massive stretches of wheatfields give way to great tracts of salt out West. The saltworks is northeast of here, on the edge of Great Blush Lake.' He waved his hand in the general direction. 'It's a salina – a salt pan. It's a sight to behold though, especially during an algal bloom. It can go bright pink – like bubble-gum. That's how it got its name – our great, blushing lake.'

Prairie was entranced by Gil's soft, deliberate way of speaking. His voice was deep, but gentle. There was none of the staccatoed authority in the way that many men spoke. Prairie suddenly longed to see the lake for herself.

'Right on our doorstep, huh?' she said, turning to Gil with a spark of joy.

Gil was still staring out into the darkness, so he did not notice. But he nodded. 'Right on our doorstep.'

○ ○ ○

Prairie woke much later than she meant to, but as she was not due to start at the exchange until six o'clock that evening, she decided to treat herself to a leisurely breakfast in the café across the road.

The *Granary Caff and Bake House* was cheery and warm, and well-patroned on this Sunday morning. Blue and white gingham tablecloths and curtains contrasted starkly with the black and white chequered floor tiles. The smell of freshly baked bread, brewed coffee and fried bacon embraced Prairie as she entered. She smiled. Her three favourite 'B's. She was liking Wheatsheaf more and more with every passing hour. The bell above the door chimed.

'Are you here for breakfast?'

'Yes, please.'

'Take a seat and someone will be right with you. Simone? *Simone!* Customer!'

Prairie took a seat by the window so she could watch Wheatsheaf go about life on this crisp Autumn morning. She picked up a menu, decided on the *'Granary Special'* without sausage and was patiently awaiting the arrival of the dutiful Simone when the couple at the next table caught her attention.

'This is far too hot! You stupid girl! I've burned my mouth!' An elderly woman draped in a fur, with her back to Prairie suddenly lashed out and struck her female companion, a woman, Prairie judged, to be anywhere between forty and fifty-five. The woman recoiled, holding her left arm. She caught Prairie's gaze and looked mortified.

'I'm sorry,' she whispered to the old woman. 'I did ask for it to be made not too hot. You should have blown on it first.'

'Do you think I have all the time in the world to wait for coffee to cool? I could be dead by dinnertime.' Prairie stifled a snigger.

'Oh Mother, please! You'll outlive me.'

''Course, I will. You're not getting my money. You needn't think you will.'

'Take some water, Mother.'

'*You* take the water!' The old woman shoved the glass at her daughter, sloshing it all over the blue gingham check.

Simone was suddenly at Prairie's side. 'Ready to order?' she asked, chewing gum like a cow toying with cud.

'Yes,' said Prairie, tearing her eyes off the next table. 'I'll have the *Granary Special* – without sausage, please.'

'But it comes with sausage,' said Simone.

'Oh! Yes, I realise that. I was wondering whether I could have the meal *without* the sausage. I don't really like them, and I wouldn't want to waste one.'

'It comes with sausage. Want to order something else?' Simone glared at her, chewing. Prairie smiled back.

'It's alright Simone,' called the lady behind the counter, 'just put the order through.' Simone sighed and turned on her heel.

The bell on the café door chimed again, and in came Constable Timms accompanied by a priest. The policeman saw Prairie, waved stiffly and nodded. The priest saw the elderly lady and her daughter and approached the table.

'Mrs Comfrey. Miss Comfrey, we missed you at Church again this morning,' he said, in a lilting cadence.

'And you can go on missing me at that pestilential shithole,' the old woman retorted.

'Mother! Please! I'm so sorry, Father Childers.'

'I'm bloody not!'

A native of West Belfast, Ernest Childers, had seen a thing or two in his time and was now, to his eternal gratitude, the parish priest at Our Lady of Perpetual Sorrow, the great Catholic edifice on the hill overlooking the town. The townsfolk called it 'Our Lady of Perpetual Embarrassment' ever since Father O'Dougherty, a visiting priest from Limerick, was caught with one hand in the offertory plate and the other down Ivy Purwell's blouse in the summer of Sixty-Three. The affair caused the archbishop himself to descend upon the town to round up his flock, making sure they didn't stray, God forbid, to the Anglican church in Blackwatch.

Father Childers smiled benignly at the old woman. 'Hopefully, you'll be able to make your way along to the confessional box soon, Mrs Comfrey. You'll be wanting to take the Host during one of our services, surely?'

'I'll take the host right up my backside, is where I'll take it. I have no sins to confess, Father. But Agnes here, I'm sure, will have much to discuss with you in there.' She laughed the hacking laugh of a crow.

'Mother!' Agnes Comfrey chided, a red rash creeping up her throat. To the priest she said, 'We'll be along as soon as we are able, Father.' The priest smiled.

'Very good, Miss Comfrey. The doors of Our Lady are always open.'

'So are Our Lady's legs!'

'Mother!'

Prairie had jammed her serviette into her mouth to keep from laughing out loud. The priest and the policeman moved to a table in the furthest corner of the restaurant, and Prairie spent the time waiting for her breakfast watching the street outside, and the Table Comfrey from the corner of her eye. But mostly the Table Comfrey and the pinched face of 'Agnes with Much to Discuss.'

○ ○ ○

After breakfast, Prairie and Baby Blue headed to the last building on Grain Street, north of the town. They pulled onto the forecourt of Reynolds Automotive to see about a new spare wheel. She didn't expect the garage to be open on a Sunday and was surprised to find the door to the office unlocked. A layer of grime covered every conceivable surface. There was nobody about.

'Hello?' Prairie called and waited a moment. When nobody answered, she gingerly turned a filthy door handle on the opposite wall and found herself inside the garage. She was about to call out again when she heard voices.

'You're a bloody idiot.' A man's voice came from within, but Prairie couldn't see the owner. 'She's a bloody prick-tease, but you won't be told.'

'I know that now.' A second voice, male, was younger.

'You want to teach it a bloody lesson, Son. I would. And no mistake.'

'Yeah. I know that now. I will.'

'Hello?' Prairie called again. A piece of metal clanged, followed by an expletive. A head popped up from underneath the bonnet of a caramel-coloured FJ Holden. Another slid out from underneath it.

'Sorry, love. Dropped me spanner,' said the bonnet-dweller. He was a grease-smeared man in his forties.

Prairie smiled, stiffly. 'I'm sorry to bother you on a Sunday. I was just after a spare wheel, for a Morris Minor. I've burst a tyre.'

Bonnet-Dweller looked her up and down and a smile played about his lips. Prairie shifted from one foot to the other. His gaze unnerved her a little.

'Sure, love. We'll be right with you.'

O   O   O

Thirty minutes later, Baby Blue purred jauntily down the highway. Prairie, although grateful for the new spare wheel, vowed never to set foot in that garage again. She could still taste the oil and grime. She turned up the radio.

On the right, as always, she passed a ramshackle homestead amongst a grove of trees, the last house in town. As she drove by the exchange on the left, she beeped the horn, just for fun. Her sketchpad slid about on the seat beside her as she rounded a great curve in the road and about seven miles later, just as he'd said, on the right there was a huge shimmering expanse, bleached white by the sun. Gil's 'great blushing lake.'

Prairie had thought of little else and longed to see the great salt basin for herself. She had hoped that Gil might suggest accompanying her there, but he had business in Golga, two hours to the north, and would be away from the town all day.

A red dirt road peeled off to the right and some bone-jarring minutes later, Prairie pulled into a small dusty carpark. She took her sketchpad and purse, locked Baby Blue and followed a narrow track down to the lake's edge. Overhead, in a perfect arc of blue, wispy cirrus clouds looked like strokes from an artist's brush on a great, blank canvas.

Prairie pushed past the low shrubs of samphire and saltbush and when she reached the shoreline, her heart leapt. She grinned so widely, her face ached. Huge, delicate crusts of salt sparkled like crystals in the sun. Further out, little islands – 'salt banks' – rose here and there amongst shimmering pools of pale pink. There was no wind. The lake was completely still, the sweep of clouds reflected in the mirror surface below. Prairie stood for a minute, her face towards the sun, and breathed deeply. A tang of briny water and a faint smell of rotting fish tickled her nostrils. She disturbed some seagulls, and they wheeled and squabbled.

Salt crunched underfoot as Prairie walked along the shore. She dared to venture too close at one point, sinking and sliding in sucking mud. She gasped and retreated up onto a dune. Upon closer examination, Prairie saw that it was a calcified hill of salt and smiled in wonder to herself. She sat down and pulled her sketchpad and a pencil out of her bag.

Blush Lake was so vast Prairie could not see its far shore. It simply melted into the horizon. Sea and sky, sky and sea, expertly blended on the artist's pallet, one reflecting the other. In the foreground, there were bursts of bright pink and dazzling shocks of white. Here and there, dead trees rose up out of the brine. Prairie began to sketch. Not another soul approached the lake and as the sun reached its zenith and commenced an arc back down the sky, she sat on the salt mound, sketching and sketching, as though she were put on the planet just to capture the lake's every mood.

4

The Night Shift

At precisely six o'clock, Prairie pushed open the door to the exchange. Olive Wellshorn was standing there in her coat, ready to go.

'Tag!' she said. 'You're it!'

Prairie laughed and hung her coat on the stand. 'Have a good night, Olive. Hello, Briar, are you well?'

Briar turned and put her finger to her lips, listening intently into her headset.

'Sorry!' mouthed Prairie. She sat down at her switchboard, and no sooner had she picked up her headset than the board lit up. She answered with 'Wheatsheaf. Number please?' and then 'Hold the line please.' She plugged in a jack, summoned the number on the rotary dial and connected the parties. She pulled a docket pad towards her and in neat blue letters, wrote down the time of the call, the caller and the number she'd connected.

'Hooly dooly,' said Briar rolling her eyes, scribbling furiously on a pad beside her. She slid the little switchboard key in front of her into its home position, pushed her headset back and turned to Prairie. 'Good evening! How was your day about Wheatsheaf? Find everything you need?'

'Oh yes,' said Prairie. 'I had breakfast at that darling little café across from the hotel.'

'The Granary? Isn't Rosie-Mandy MacMurrough a complete sweetheart? But that Simone of hers…ugh!' Briar rolled her eyes again.

Prairie smiled. 'She's a stickler for the rules when it comes to sausage!'

Briar had taken a sip of water and spat it across the switchboard. This made the girls laugh harder. 'Rosie dropped her on her head when she was a baby!' said Briar, wiping her eyes and dabbing at the water. Prairie stopped laughing.

'Really?'

Briar nodded. 'Oh yes. It was the talk of the town for a week. They didn't think she'd live. But here she is, darkening the doorknob of every coffee cup in the Granary.'

Prairie's switch lit up. She lunged for her headset. 'Wheatsheaf. Number please? Certainly, hold the line please.' She dialled the number and connected the call, completed her docket fastidiously and turned to Briar. 'In the café, there were two ladies, a mother and daughter. I'm sure the priest said Comfrey…'

'Ugh,' sniffed Briar, eyes rolling some more. 'That Gwinny Comfrey is a vexatious old witch. I don't know how Agnes stands it. I'd have put a pillow over that hateful old sow's head years ago.'

'Agnes is the daughter?'

Briar nodded. 'Uh-huh. God knows how she stays. The 'why' is obvious, of course – money. The old bag is rumoured to be sitting on a fortune but she's so miserly and treats Agnes appallingly. Won't let her have a cent until she's dead, I believe.' She snorted. 'Gwinny looks set to outlive us all!'

'How old is Agnes?' asked Prairie. She couldn't stop thinking about the cruel way Gwinny had struck her daughter in the café.

'Dunno. Thirty-five? Sixty? Who can say? She does nothing to make herself look attractive.' The console lit up. Briar pounced. 'Wheatsheaf. Number please? Hold the line please.'

Prairie watched her dial the number and connect the call. She pulled her notepad close, put her finger to her lips, and pushed the little switchboard key in front of her forward, slowly and carefully so as not to make a sound. Prairie was astonished. The only time Prairie ever pushed that key forward – to listen in on a call – was when she was an overseer, auditing the performance of the lines. She sat silently, praying her switchboard would not light up, until Briar lowered the switch key again and whipped off her headset.

'Oh, my giddy aunt! Prunella Battersby just spent that entire phone call complaining to Irma Vickery – she's the owner of *Haughty Couture*, the dress shop in town – that the dress she wore to her husband's dinner-dance last night ripped in the seat when she sat down to dinner! Can you believe it?' Briar rocked with laughter.

'Who's Prunella Battersby?' asked Prairie.

'Ich,' Briar wrinkled her nose by way of response. 'She's the worst. Her husband owns *Battersby's Meats* – the abattoir in Dumbogan. They live here for some reason, but she thinks she's way too good for the rest of us. Wish she'd just piss off up to Golga.' The switch lit up. Prairie was quick to intervene. 'Want a cuppa?' asked Briar, rising from her seat. 'T or C?'

'C please,' said Prairie, scribbling on a docket. It was drafty in the exchange. She made a mental note to bring in the picnic rug from Baby Blue for future shifts. 'Do you often listen in on calls,' she asked casually, as Briar set down a steaming mug of coffee in front of her. Briar shrugged, taking a sip of tea.

'Occasionally. When the mood takes me. It's the telephonist's prerogative to know what's going on in the town, wouldn't you say?'

Prairie sipped, swallowed and answered carefully. 'I wouldn't say that. No. It's eavesdropping.'

'We all do it,' said Briar defensively. 'How else would we know who's having affairs and who's having abortions?'

'Why would you want to know that?' Prairie was incredulous. 'You'd look at the whole town differently.'

'Honey, you're here for a good time – not a long time,' Briar replied, turning back to her switchboard and donning her headphones. 'This isn't the Big Smoke.' She said little after that. The exchange was suddenly very cool indeed.

5

Dust

Prairie slept until eight o'clock on Monday morning, her day off. She pulled her dressing gown on over her nightie, gathered her towel and toiletries, and slipped out onto the balcony to watch Wheatsheaf waking up.

The sky was blue and cloudless, but the air was crisp. She shivered and clutched her belongings close – perfect bath weather. She hoped it was free. She looked down at the shops lining the other side of the street: the green grocer's, *Battersby's Meats*, the *Granary Caff and Bake House*, Irma Vickery's *Haughty Couture*. Away down to the left was a lamppost with a blue light and Constable Timm's patrol car parked in the driveway. On the opposite corner was the red brick Post Office.

Prairie was about to turn away when the sight of a lonely figure carrying a shopping bag in each hand caught her gaze. Agnes Comfrey had stepped out of the grocer's and now stared across at the Harvest Hotel. She seemed to catch the eye of Prairie just for a moment. Prairie raised her hand instinctively, but Agnes turned and began to trudge up the street towards the Post Office and Police Station, listing side to side under the weight of the shopping bags.

'Morning Sleepy-Head,' said Felice brightly when Prairie came downstairs. 'Want me to do you a special fry-up?'

'No thanks, Felice. I'll just have toast and coffee.'

'Right you are.' Felice was dusting the glass of a picture frame.

'What's that?' asked Prairie, as Felice moved to re-position it behind the bar.

'This?' She brought it over to the table. Prairie stared down at the framed sepia photograph. A great cloud rolled like a tidal wave over a barren landscape. 'That was the dust storm that hit us two years ago.'

'Oh my,' gasped Prairie. 'Sixty-Five? I remember that. I thought the world was going to end that day. I was down south in the city. Everything just stopped. It was two o'clock in the afternoon, but everything went dark. We were cleaning dust off everything for days.'

'Imagine what it was like up here!' said Felice, shaking her head. 'We were in the thick of it! I reckon I had dust with every meal for a good six months. The drought had been so bad up here for a couple of years before Sixty-Five. All the topsoil was loose anyway, cos nothing was growing, and when we got that northerly, bam! It was like Dustbowl America during the Depression.' She laughed but stopped abruptly. 'I don't know why I'm laughing. Things are still pretty bad up here. Rain will follow the plough? I don't think so. It's a chill wind that blows no ill.'

'An ill wind that blows no good,' said Prairie without thinking.

Felice looked at her askance. 'Of course it does, my pet, that's just what I said.' She patted Prairie's shoulder.

Prairie stared down at the picture and imagined what it must have been like, watching the great wall of dust roll over Grain Street from her hotel room window. The cloud was miles high and as dense as fog. The people of Wheatsheaf would have been terrified, not knowing when or if they'd emerge from that wall of grit; cars, buildings and livestock sand-blasted for hours.

'Agnes Comfrey,' Prairie began.

'Yes?' Felice replied through pursed red lips.

'I saw her this morning, carrying shopping home. Where does she live?'

Felice sighed. 'The Comfreys live on that property just out of town. You'd pass it every day on your way to the exchange. Where the road curves to the left, if you look to your right, it's that house there. Probably didn't notice it for all the trees.'

'Oh, my goodness,' said Prairie. 'That's quite a walk with groceries.'

Felice shrugged. 'I don't know why she was walking. They have a car.'

'Her mother,' Prairie began, but Felice interjected.

'That hateful old crone. I don't know how poor Agnes has put up with her all these years.'

'Is it age that's made her nasty?' asked Prairie. 'I saw her strike Agnes in the café. And she was terribly rude to the priest. Although -'

'Although?' Felice cocked her head.

'Some of the things she said were so over the top, I almost burst out laughing.' Prairie covered her mouth.

'Poor Father Childers,' Felice clucked. 'Don't know how he's managed to live down that debacle with Father O'Dougherty, filthy beggar. No, Gwinny Comfrey has been a wrong'un ever since I've known her. I should have gone to school with Agnes – we're about the same age, but Gwinny kept her home. Damn shame that. Agnes's nice enough. A bit timid, but I s'pose that's to be expected when you don't socialise much.'

'Do they come to town often?' asked Prairie.

'When they need to. Agnes comes more so than Gwinny; she goes to church every now and then, although I haven't seen her there for a couple of weeks. They never set foot in here. I'm sure they regard my pub as a *den of inequality,*' she laughed at her own, muddled joke. 'I'll hang this back up and get your brekkie.'

Prairie stared at the rolling wall of dust.

○   ○   ○

The *Granary Caff and Bakery* was warm and as always, smelled delicious. Simone, behind the counter, saw Prairie enter and scuttled out the back. To the right of the cash register, a tall glass case displayed some of the most mouth-watering cakes Prairie had ever seen. There was a glistening chocolate gateau (a 'gatox,' as Felice would say), a gorgeous pink creation topped with sugar-glazed strawberries, a cinnamon teacake, and several darling little cupcakes with pastel-coloured icing.

'Something take your fancy?' Rosie-Mandy was at the counter. 'My Simone makes all these.' Prairie looked up astonished and then blushed slightly. 'She a right dab hand with a cake batter,' Rosie-Mandy went on. 'And a steady hand with the icing sleeve. Goodness, I'd shake so much I'd have to pass the cake off as an abstract piece of art.' She smiled. Prairie beamed back.

'They're all beautiful. I'll take that one, please.' She pointed to a soft sponge, filled with cream and topped with pale yellow passionfruit icing.

'Good choice,' said Rosie-Mandy. 'I'll pop it into a box for you.'

With the cake nestled on the front seat beside her, Prairie nudged Baby Blue out of town. She passed Constable Timms on his way somewhere, beeped the horn at him and waved out the window. He looked around, astonished, saw Prairie, smoothed his uniform and waved back, stiffly.

'Perhaps he's more used to people throwing other things out of car windows,' she said aloud to Baby Blue and laughed.

About half a mile past Reynolds' Automotive, the road curved to the left. As Felice had said, the ramshackle property shrouded by trees loomed on the right. Prairie suddenly felt nervous. What right did she have to intrude, uninvited, onto the property of people she'd never formally met?

Prairie swung Baby Blue onto the sandy driveway and followed it underneath a canopy of dark trees to the house. She sat with Baby Blue idling, wondering whether to reverse straight back out the way she'd come, when a face at the window left her no option but to push ahead with her plan. She switched off the engine and grabbed her purse. The face at the window belonged to Agnes Comfrey, and it looked horrified. Prairie stepped out of the car and waved slightly. Agnes dropped the curtain. Prairie exhaled, smoothed her dress, walked around to the passenger door and collected the boxed cake from the seat. Steadying her nerves with more deep breaths, she mounted the rickety steps to a large veranda, which surrounded the house on two sides that Prairie could see.

The old farmhouse was weatherboard. Its yellow paint had long ago faded and was flaking in places. Some of the boards were rotten and needed replacing. The crash of piano keys could be heard from within. Taking another deep breath and balancing the cake box in her left hand, Prairie grabbed hold of the cord attached to the bell and rang the clapper. The piano stopped. There was silence, then footsteps approached the door. It squeaked on its hinges as it opened a fraction, and the space was filled by Agnes Comfrey.

'Yes?' she asked. Her face was blank.

'Oh hello,' Prairie began. *And now what?* she thought. *You haven't thought this through, have you?* 'I…my name is Prairie. Prairie Humble. I'm new to town. I'm working at the exchange – there's a vacancy there and I'm just filling in…' Silence. The expression didn't change, so she went on. 'I drive past every day, on my way to work. And I saw you this morning, and…' *And what, Prairie Humble?* she silently scolded herself. *I was spying on you in the café and I saw your mother strike you and I thought you were pitiful and then I was spying again as you carried two bags of shopping home on foot and I have no idea what I think a cake is going to fix, but here it is?*

They both looked down at the box in her hands. 'I thought the cakes in the bakery looked divine, but I can't justify buying one just for me. I'd never eat it on my own, but I thought…I thought perhaps you and your mother might like a sponge. It's passionfruit. I understand Simone bakes them fresh….'

'Simone MacMurrough is a dolt!' Gwinny Comfrey screeched from inside. 'She's a luddite! I wouldn't eat *shit* that girl has touched. Now *piss off!*'

'Mother, please!' Agnes's face reddened. 'Thank you, Miss Humble, but could you see yourself off the property please?' Her voice had an urgency to it that startled Prairie and before she could respond, the door slammed in her face. Prairie stared down at the box in her hands. She suddenly wanted to hurl it against the door. Her eyes grew hot. Shamed, she set the box on the doorstep and hurried down the steps as fast as she could without tripping on them. She gunned the engine of Baby Blue and reversed down the driveway, not looking back at the house.

When she reached the road, she drove away from Wheatsheaf, out past the exchange, towards the lake where she parked and let the tears spill out between her lashes. What had she done? How could such a kind gesture fail so miserably? She reached into her handbag for a handkerchief, wiped her eyes and blew her nose. She checked her face in the rear-view mirror. She touched up her mascara, grabbed her coat and her sketchbook and stormed down through the saltbush.

Cotton ball clouds clumped together over the horizon. Prairie sat on her mound of salt and stared out over the blushing lake. For such a huge expanse, there was not a great deal of water in it, not compared to other lakes. She closed her eyes and tried to imagine what it would have been like on the day of the dust storm. The baking temperature would have dried the lake of any moisture. In her mind's eye, she could see the cracks and fissures of the parched lakebed. She imagined the wind whipping salt and dust against anything that stood in its path, and how that must sting, to be pebble-dashed relentlessly. And she began to sketch, not the clouds now gathering on the horizon, or the blackened trees out in the shallows, or the samphire along the shore, but a great, roiling wall of dust, rolling along a barren landscape, devouring everything in its path, smothering the town. She tried to blot out the agitated face of Agnes Comfrey and dampen the ugly voice of her mother.

She didn't hear the car pull into the parking lot or the crunch of footsteps along the salty path. She was only aware of his presence when he spoke.

'You're quite good at that.'

Prairie jumped, her pencil shooting off the edge of the page. 'Oh, my goodness, you startled me!' she said, looking up at Gil Sanders, her heart pounding. 'I thought you'd still be in Golga.'

'I'm sorry,' said Gil, and held up both hands. 'I came back early. I was on my way into Wheatsheaf and saw your car. Thought I'd come and say 'Hi.' You found this place alright then?'

'Yes,' said Prairie, willing her heart to slow down. 'It's achingly beautiful here. So peaceful – and pink! I've never seen anything like it. Thank you for sharing its secret with me.'

'Ah,' said Gil, conspiratorially. 'This is a beautiful vantage point, but the whole town gets to see this. If it's a secret vista you're after, I can show you one that'll make you want to fill that whole sketch book. Follow me to the saltworks and I'll take you to a lookout point I bet nobody in the town has ever seen. Unless they work at Blush Salt, of course,' he added as an after-thought and laughed. Prairie found herself laughing too. What a difference an hour had made to her mood.

6
Salt

Prairie followed Gil's silver Kingswood station wagon up the highway until it turned right onto the aptly named Saltworks Road. They were waved through a boom gate manned by a security guard, and Gil pulled into a parking lot. Prairie parked next to him and wound down her window as he approached.

'You can either ride with me, or I'll ride with you?' he said.

'Hop in!' Prairie leaned across to unlock the passenger door. Gil slid in beside her. The scent of his cologne filled the car. Following his directions, Prairie drove past an administration building and towards a series of large square pools.

'What are they?' she asked.

'These are salt pans,' Gil explained. 'We harvest salt from them – to sell.'

Huge pieces of machinery were hard at work as they drove past. The road curved around to the right and followed the shore of the lake for about half a mile. 'Park here,' Gil eventually indicated. 'Are your shoes good for walking?' Prairie showed him her grey flats and he smiled approvingly. He held out his hand, offering to help her from the car. She didn't need help, but she took his hand anyway, hers feeling tiny and delicate in his huge palm.

He led her a little way down towards the shore and then picked up a narrow path that climbed a cliff that curved around the edge of the lake. The upwards climb set Prairie's heart racing, and she tried not to breathe like a labouring sow. To her great relief, they soon came to an outcrop that looked out over a huge expanse of the lake, shimmering in the sun like a shard of rose quartz.

'It's beautiful!' Prairie gasped. There was just enough water in the lake to hint at its rosy hue, but she could see that great tracts of it were dry and encrusted with pink salt crystals. Looking down, she saw a boardwalk leading into the lake.

'You can walk right out onto it?' she asked.

Gil nodded. 'And I frequently do. I use it to get samples. The water is little more than shin deep most times. Look out there,' he said, pointing to the far shore. Clouds were gathering in a grey bank, turning the further, deeper parts of the lake the colour of rose. 'I hope it rains,' he said. 'She takes on a whole 'nother aspect when she's full. Like a mirror to the sky. Wonderful photography.'

Hand in hand, Gil led Prairie carefully down the sandy trail to the edge of the boardwalk. 'I've never seen anything like this in my whole life,' Prairie breathed, shielding her eyes from the glare.

'They are remarkable things,' said Gil.

'How ever did it get here?' she wondered. 'I bet this is what it looks like on the surface of the Moon.'

'This whole area is a depression' he went on. 'It's just a shallow basin. Thousands of years ago, it would probably have been a tributary of the Golga River. But over time, huge sand drifts coming from the west blocked the tributary's natural passage. The salina is still being fed by underground water, of course, but the water-table is shallow – by that I mean it runs close to the surface. Because it's so hot up here much of the year, evaporation happens far quicker than the rain can fall. So, you get the minerals that create salt crystals leaching up when it's wet and drying out in the sun.' He leaned down and scooped up a handful of white powdery crystals and held his palm out to Prairie. 'Taste it,' he said. She dipped her index finger in the gritty substance and tentatively licked it with the tip of her tongue.

'Wow!' she said. 'That's salty, alright.'

'It's incredibly concentrated,' Gil explained. 'Eight hundred times saltier than the sea. We harvest one of the purest forms of salt in Australia out here.'

They strolled out onto the boardwalk, Prairie marvelling at the pockets of bright pink water in between the crusty islands of salt. 'Why is the lake pink?' she asked, fascinated.

'I'm glad you asked,' said Gil. Clearly, he was passionate about his work and was enjoying having an audience. Prairie was content to let him explain. 'Salinity – saltiness – is the perfect condition for certain types of algae. The algae here are 'extremophiles' – organisms that live in great extremes of temperature. When the weather conditions are just right, algae in the saltwater produce red carotenoids. It's like they're using a sunscreen. The carotenoids make sure the algae don't burn while they photosynthesise. When we get an algal bloom, the whole lake turns bubble-gum pink. I hope you get to see it one day.'

They turned and walked back to the shore. *I hope I do too,* thought Prairie.

'There are other pink lakes, northwest of here. Maybe on your next day off, we could go for a drive?' Gil asked hopefully.

'How far away are they?'

'A couple of hours? We could take a picnic. Lots of flies out there and saltbush, but there are some pretty views.'

'Sure,' said Prairie brightly, mentally running through her shifts to calculate her next day off. 'What on earth is that?' she said, pointing to a little ball attached to a vine snaking across the ground. She bent closer to inspect it. 'Is that a watermelon?'

'No,' said Gil. 'Never eat one. They're bitter. And they're a pest. It's an Afghan melon. Salt harvesting in the region began during the First World War – by hand. Could you imagine that? No form of mechanical harvesting out here on these pans in a hundred-degree heat?'

'I'd die!'

'Many did, I suppose. The glare is blinding in Summer. I can only stay out in short bursts. Workers broke the salt up with picks and then shovelled it by hand into wheelbarrows. Then they had to wheel the barrows across wooden planks to the shore.'

'Bugger that!' said Prairie, and Gil laughed.

'Later on, they used scarifiers, a kind of scraper-thing, drawn by horses – much easier to break up the salt using horsepower than a man with a pick or shovel.'

'Those poor horses!' Prairie exclaimed and Gil didn't disagree.

'Later still, they brought camel trains and their Afghan drivers down from Broken Hill. We think the drivers brought these melons as food for the camels.' They were walking back to the car now.

'How long have you worked here, Gil?' Prairie asked, picking her way carefully along the path. She liked the way her shoes crunched the salt underfoot.

'I've been coming down on and off for about two years,' he said. 'The business is booming. We're looking to expand – creating a few more harvesting pans to keep up with the demand. There're a few blockers though.'

'Blockers?'

'Neighbouring farms,' said Gil. 'Salt's a precious commodity. But so are wheat and lamb.'

'I feel like a roast dinner now,' said Prairie, laughing.

'Me too,' said Gil. Baby Blue was now in sight. 'Say, could I take you to dinner one night? I know a local place that does a great lamb roast?'

'Would that be the Harvest Hotel?' Prairie asked, playfully putting a finger to her chin.

'You got it in one!' Gil laughed with her. She loved the way his eyes sparkled. *Sky mirrors,* she thought happily and looked forward to dinner time.

O   O   O

'Wheatsheaf. Number please?' Briar snapped impatiently. 'Hold the line please.' She connected the call, wrote the time, name and number on a docket and rubbed her right heel. A puffy sac of liquid bounced under the light pressure of her finger. She winced and felt sick.

'How are your feet now?' asked Olive.

'Rubbed raw. Think I'll stick them in another bucket of water.'

'Serves you right for wearing those stupid shoes all the time. They're ridiculous.'

'*They* are the height of fashion,' Briar retorted. 'You should open a magazine every now and then, Olive dear. You've had the same hairstyle since Nineteen Fifty-Seven.'

Olive rolled her eyes and went to the little tearoom. 'You didn't even know me in Nineteen Fifty-Seven,' she called, switching the electric kettle on. 'Want a cuppa? I think I'll have one more before I go.' It was dark and the cold had well and truly set in.

'Yes please, Olive dear. Ughh! These damn calls.' A light flickered and she lunged for her headset. 'Wheatsheaf. Number please?'

'Hello, I need a number in Melbourne please.' Briar didn't recognise the voice. She reached for her docket, plugged in the jack and dialled the number. The call rang out. 'That line isn't answering, Sir.'

'Can you try another?'

Briar scribbled the number down and connected the jack. She dialled a second time and waited for the tone. A voice answered. 'Call from Wheatsheaf,' she told the recipient. 'Go ahead caller,' she said, quietly sliding the key forward.

7
Death: Part 1

The sun was rising as Prairie's Tuesday shift got underway. The sky was a brilliant red, a warning to shepherds and sailors everywhere. It was stuffy in the exchange – Matthew Vallen, the night boy, had been there since ten o'clock the previous evening. He'd defied Mr Peterson's orders and left the radiator on all night.

Prairie had risen early. She dressed and drove to the exchange in darkness, knowing the sun would be making its grand appearance in less than half an hour. She longed to drive straight past the red brick building and out to the salt pan to watch the great red fireball crest the horizon. She thought of Gil and smiled. She'd do that tomorrow, perhaps? Definitely on her next day off. Maybe she could convince Gil to come too? She'd kept her eyes firmly on the road as she passed the Comfrey homestead. The sting of embarrassment was still fierce.

Don't let it eat at you, Gil had said, when she told him about the passionfruit sponge. *You did a nice thing. Some people just don't deserve nice.*

At fifteen minutes past eight, Matthew was still slumped over his switchboard, oblivious to the coffee Prairie had poured him an hour ago. She let him sleep. They were awful shifts. At the sound of a car on the gravel outside, Prairie went to the window. Mr Peterson's black Hillman was pulling into the exchange's driveway.

'Matt!' she hissed. 'Get up! It's Mr Peterson.'

'What?' Matthew raised his head wearily and wiped some drool from the corner of his mouth. His eyes were red-rimmed.

'Mr Peterson!' she said deliberately. 'You'd better go splash some cold water on your face. Hurry! He'll be inside in a minute.' Matthew disentangled himself from his headset and lurched from his chair.

'Can you switch the radiator off?' he asked. Prairie nodded.

Fidel Peterson stomped up the steps to his exchange and turned his key in the lock. Only Olive, as the second in charge, had an extra set of keys. Working continuous rotating shifts, it was always expected that the outgoing shift would let the oncoming shift in. Prairie turned in her seat, headset neatly positioned, pen poised to complete a docket.

'Mr Peterson!' she exclaimed with mock surprise. 'Good morning!'

'Good morning, Miss Humble,' he grumbled and then pulled at his collar. 'By God, it's like a sauna in here!'

'Oh,' Prairie put her hand to her mouth. 'I'm sorry Mr Peterson – it was so cold when I arrived at dawn. I'm afraid I've probably turned the radiator up a tad too high.'

Peterson looked at his watch. It was half past eight. 'Yes, well.'

The switch lit up. *Blink. Blink. Blink.* Prairie deftly turned her attention to the call.

'Wheatsheaf. Number please? Certainly Miss Vickery. Hold the line please.' She plugged in her jacks, filled in the docket and turned her attention back to Mr Peterson. He looked at his watch again and turned towards his small office.

'What do you say to a nice cup of tea, Miss Humble?'

'I'd *love* one, Mr Peterson. You are very kind to offer. White with one please.' *Blink. Blink. Blink.* 'Wheatsheaf. Number please?' Prairie didn't dare turn to face him. She stared straight ahead, focussed on her task, afraid she'd burst into laughter otherwise. Fidel Peterson bristled slightly, but dutifully went to the tearoom.

Mabel Wattage had barely taken off her hat and coat when Peterson asked to see her in his office.

'What have I done?' she whispered to Prairie. 'What does he want?'

Prairie shrugged, bewildered. 'I've no idea. He's not said a word, except to complain about the heat and ask for a cup of tea. Are you alright?'

Mabel's face was ashen. 'I suspect I'm not about to be.' She smoothed her pale peach dress, squared her shoulders, combed stray hair from her face and entered Peterson's office. She was ushered into a seat and the door was shut behind her. Prairie pushed back her headset slightly, and then pushed it off altogether so it hung about her shoulders. Fidel Peterson's voice was muffled behind the door. Prairie strained to make out words here and there, and then chided herself. *Prairie Humble, you are no better than Briar Lee.* She could hear Mabel's voice rising. She was protesting something. Peterson was trying to placate her.

'*I will not lower my voice!*' came through the door audibly enough. Someone slammed the desk and then Prairie thought she heard sobbing. She pulled her headset back on just as the door flew open and Mabel Wattage stood in its frame, tears streaming down her reddened face. She held a crumpled tissue to her nose. Fidel Peterson hovered uncomfortably behind her.

'He's fired me!' she sobbed, looking straight at Prairie. 'The bloody bastard's gone and fired me.'

'Miss Wattage, now please!'

'*Oh, go fuck yourself, Fidel!*' Mabel roared. She turned on her heel, grabbed her hat and coat, and slammed the exchange door as hard as she could behind her. The windows rattled in their frames. Peterson cringed as an engine gunned and revved outside.

'I wouldn't stand there, Sir,' said Prairie gravely. 'Mabel might be fixing to drive right through that wall.'

Fidel Peterson looked at Prairie startled. 'Yes, well. Thank you, Miss Humble. I'm afraid I've had to let Miss Wattage go.'

'So I gathered,' Prairie's face was calm, but she did not smile. Much to her relief, the switch lit up. 'Wheatsheaf. Number please?' she said quietly into the headset.

○ ○ ○

'I can't believe it. I just can't believe it,' Mabel sniffed. Prairie laid her hand on top of Mabel's. It was shaking. After her shift, Prairie found Mabel Wattage sitting in the *Granary Caff*. She'd called in for a sandwich and saw the hunched form of Mabel sitting at a table in the far corner, her back to the window, quietly sobbing. Rosie-Mandy jerked her head towards Mabel when Prairie approached the counter.

'Been here all morning,' she whispered. 'Simone's taken three cups of tea over and she's let each one go cold. What on earth's wrong with her?'

'I'm not sure,' said Prairie. 'Could I have a coffee and sand-wich – to have here please, Rosie?'

She made her way over to the table and placed her hand gently on Mabel's shoulder. Mabel stiffened. Prairie looked down at her tear-streaked face. 'May I?' she asked quietly, pulling out a chair. Mabel's eyes filled with tears all over again, but she nodded slowly. 'Oh Mabel, darling. It's breaking my heart to see you like this. What on earth happened?'

'Didn't that fat bastard tell you?' Mabel sniffed. She picked up her teacup and brought it to her lips but plonked it down on the saucer without taking a sip.

Prairie let out a sympathetic snort. 'He is a little overweight, isn't he? But sadly, he doesn't gossip.' Mabel smiled, in spite of herself. 'Oh, do tell me what's happened, Mabel? Maybe we can find a way to fix things?'

Mabel shook her head sadly. 'No, I'm afraid he has me bang to rights. I can't fix this.' She said nothing more. Prairie sat there help-lessly. Simone brought over a mug of coffee and a ham sandwich.

'Are you wanting another tea?' she asked bluntly, staring at Mabel.

'No thank you, Simone,' Mabel replied without looking up. She sat staring into space. After a while, very quietly, she said 'I just don't understand. Nobody knew. Nobody knows. How could *he* know?'

Prairie leaned forward. 'Know what, Mabel dear?'

Mabel raised her mournful gaze to meet Prairie's eyes. 'You're so kind to be concerned for me, Prairie. I knew you were a kind person, the minute I met you. I'll miss working alongside you.' She sighed. Prairie put down her sandwich. Her appetite was long gone. 'I have a son.' Mabel's voice was barely a whisper. 'Eamon. He's seven. He lives with my sister and her husband, in Golga.'

'Oh Mabel,' Prairie felt her eyes prickle with tears.

'I paid the price for letting my emotions run away with me. His father didn't want to know. It's so easy for them, isn't it? He'll go on to be some high-flying pillar of the community and I'm forced to leave the Postmaster General because technically, I should be married. We all know that a married woman loses her ability to do anything other than run a household as soon as she puts that ring on her finger. Brain goes to mush apparently. I wouldn't know. I'm worse than *not married*, because I had a child out of wedlock. A beautiful, bright boy that I've had to keep hidden, so I can keep working to earn money to pay for his upkeep, for my board, for the trips back and forth to Golga. And now I don't have anything.' Her face crumpled and a great wracking sob ripped through her.

Sympathetic tears trickled down either side of Prairie's nose. Hot, salty tears for the second day in a row. This saline land was turning her to salt too. 'It's a damned stupid rule,' she said, through gritted teeth.

Mabel wiped her face with her napkin and then twisted it in her hands. 'I just don't understand how Peterson found out. Bastard wouldn't tell me. I haven't heard boo from Eamon's father since I decided to keep him. He would have had me up the clinic in a flash, but I refused. I took an extended holiday to Golga when I was six months gone and stayed with Elsie – that's my sister – until after he was born. I came back as soon as my milk had dried up. I told no one. Nobody but my sister and brother-in-law know. How on *earth* did Peterson find out?'

Prairie thought for a moment. 'Do you ever call Eamon?' she asked gently.

Mabel sniffed. 'Oh yes,' she said brightly, through her tears. 'I call him every night at seven o'clock when I'm not on nightshift. He tells me all about his day.'

Unease filled the pit in Prairie's stomach.

O　　O　　O

The bar at the Harvest Hotel was crowded, and Prairie had to push her way through with the drinks. She set them down in front of Olive and Briar – soda and lime for Olive, who was due to commence work at six, and a glass of Chablis for Briar, who was not due to commence anything. Prairie had a glass of Guinness. Following the afternoon with Mabel, she wanted to drink it by the pint. Outside, the wind was blowing fiercely.

'I don't envy you having to go out in that, Olive,' she said, listening to it whistling through the gaps in the doors and windows.

'I'd give anything to be on a Caribbean island right now,' Olive murmured, sucking through a straw. 'Peterson called me this morning to tell me he was letting Mabel go. I just can't believe it. That's another slot we're going to have to fill. Do you think you could handle the shift solo tomorrow, Prair, worst case scenario if I can't get one of the Night Boys to cover?'

'If Mr Peterson sacked Mabel, I think *he* should have to cover the shift,' Briar quipped as she delicately sipped her Chablis.

Prairie regarded the girl over the rim of her beer glass. 'Of course, Olive, no problem,' she said.

'Did Peterson say why he sacked her?' asked Briar. Olive shook her head.

'No. He was very tight-lipped. Just said he had to let her go and that was an end to it.'

'How about you, Prair?' Briar turned her luminous blue eyes towards Prairie. 'You would've heard something, being on shift this morning. Surely?'

Prairie took a deep draught of the dark stout and licked the froth from her lip. 'I didn't hear a thing,' she said and changed the subject. 'What did you do with your day off, Briar?'

'Oh, picked up my stupid car from Reynolds' Auto – they had to charge my battery after it died the other day. And then I *shopped* until I *da-ropped*,' she said and brought a small parcel out of her bag. 'I bought this!' She unwrapped a silver bracelet in front of them. It was studded with tiny diamonds.

Olive whistled. 'That's perty.'

'Isn't it?' gushed Briar. 'I've had my eye on it for weeks! Billie Jean King wore one just like it during the semi-finals of the US Open last year. When I saw it in the window of Evans & Son, I just *had* to have it.' She rewrapped the bracelet and put it away. 'I saw that Dag-nes Comfrey in Carlson's, too,' she said, sipping her drink.

'Oh?' said Prairie, 'What was she doing in there?' She had been trying not to think about the Comfreys. Briar shrugged, disinterested.

'Dunno. Buying a new frying pan, I guess.'

'Hey Prairie!' Gil was suddenly at the table. She looked up at him and he laughed. Briar made a 'moustache' gesture with her finger.

'Oh!' Prairie gasped and wiped her mouth hurriedly. Gil laughed harder and that made her laugh too.

'Another drink?' he asked. Prairie shook her head.

'No, thank you.'

'Ladies?'

Olive declined the invitation. 'Next time, maybe? Right now, I have to run,' she said, draining the last drops of her soda. 'You can have my seat, Gil. Ladies, see you later. Prairie, thanks so much for agreeing to work later tomorrow – I'll be in touch. Hopefully, we can work something out soon.'

'No problem.'

Briar regarded the liquid in her glass carefully before concluding she had a sufficient quantity left. 'Not for me, thanks Gil. Here,' she patted the vacated seat coquettishly. 'Come sit by me and tell me all about yourself. Prairie's been keeping you quite the secret and I want to know all about it.' She flashed Prairie a sly grin and raised her glass.

'I have not,' said Prairie hotly.

'Oh, come now,' Briar teased. 'Trips out to the big ol' lake? Tell me Gil, how is the salt business doing these days?' Prairie thought she detected a flush of colour in Gil's cheeks. He was clearly uncomfortable.

Damn you, Briar Lee, she thought. Prairie sipped her drink to keep her mouth occupied.

'Umm, it's doing quite well, I suppose,' Gil replied. 'Our yield has been pretty substantial the past couple of years.'

'I suppose the drought helped with that?' said Briar, sipping away.

At least she's stopped pouting ridiculously, Prairie thought.

'Not the drought, per se,' said Gil thoughtfully. 'The warmer weather, certainly. We need the sun to evaporate the brine to form salt crystals, but we also need the groundwater to come to the surface bringing the minerals with it. I'm afraid that doesn't happen during a drought. The water table recedes far too low.'

'Fascinating,' said Briar, insincerely, twirling her glass. 'Tell me Gil, are the salt works planning to expand at all?' It was an odd question. Gil was thrown.

'Expand? How do you mean? More staff?'

The conversation was cut short by the sound of the pub door being thrown open and shrieks from the front of the bar. Something heavy thudded to the floor and people standing at the bar leapt out of the way.

'Look what those bastards have done!' roared a man's voice.

'What is it?' said Briar, leaping up out of her chair, straining to see through the commotion. The crowd backed away and Prairie caught a glimpse of something white on the floor of the bar. It looked like a blanket.

'What is it, Gil?' she asked.

'Oh God!' Gil recoiled. 'It's a sheep! He's brought a dead sheep in here.'

'Ewww!'

'What the *hell* are you doing, Heck? Get that flamin' thing out of here,' thundered Arthur Banbury. 'Right *now!*'

'No!' said Heck Johnson, defiant. 'Not til youse have all seen what they're doing to me. What they're doing to all us farmers 'round here.'

'Who's doing what, Heck?' said Felice, trying to calm the situation.

'Those salt bastards, that's who.' Looking around the crowd, Heck Johnson locked eyes with Gil and raised a finger, pointing directly at him. 'You! You salt bastard! You killed twenty head of my sheep! All of 'em dead in the bottom paddock.'

Prairie looked at Gil. He was ashen. 'I haven't killed anything!' he protested. His face had gone as white as the dead sheep before him.

'*Poisoned 'em!* Just so you can get your hands on my land! Well, let me tell you something, son. You bastards had better poison *me* an' all before I'll let that happen!'

'Come on, Heck, let's be having you.' Constable Timms was suddenly front and centre, calmly restoring order to his town.

'Get off me, Timms. It's *him* who wants arresting.' Heck Johnson jabbed a gnarled finger at Gil again.

'Nobody's getting arrested *yet*. But if you don't come quietly, Heck, I'll be taking *you* out in cuffs. Come *on!*'

'This isn't the last you'll hear of this,' the sun-leathered farmer warned as he turned to leave. 'All of youse, mark my words,' he said, menacingly pointing his finger at the by-standers. 'Wheat'll give way to salt if these bastards have their way. And we'll all be on the breadline. *With no bloody wheat to make the bread!*'

'Come on,' said Timms, more forcefully now, his hand on Heck Johnson's shoulder, pushing him towards the door.

'*Someone get that bloody sheep off my floor!*' roared Arthur.

8
Death: Part 2

News of Hector Johnson's dead sheep raced through Wheatsheaf like fire in a field. It was all the town could talk about. When Prairie came downstairs for breakfast, Felice was on the phone in the bar. She overheard the words *'dead,' 'melee'* (which Felice pronounced 'melly') and *'salt people.'* She looked around for Gil, but the hotel was empty. He'd been shaken last night in the wake of Heck Johnson's accusations.

'I'm sure nobody will take any notice,' Prairie had told him afterwards, as they looked out across the wind-whipped town from the balcony. They'd retreated up there as soon as the crowd had dissipated, eager to distance themselves from the ugly scene.

'This is a small town, Prairie. And small-town people thrive on gossip. Mud, as they say, has a terrible habit of sticking.'

'Why would anyone think you'd poison Hector Johnson's sheep, Gil? The idea is just preposterous!'

'They'd think it because *he* thinks it. He's a well-respected member of the farming community around here. His word may as well be gospel.'

Prairie thought for a moment. 'But why would *he* think it, Gil?'

Gil shrugged. 'Hector Johnson's farm is the closest property to the land occupied by Blush Salt. I expect he thinks nobody but someone from Blush Salt would have cause to be in his bottom paddock.' He looked at Prairie and his eyes hardened. 'I didn't do it, Prairie. I didn't poison Heck's sheep.'

Prairie laid a hand on his arm. 'I believe that Gil, with my whole heart.'

His eyes softened and he stared back out into the darkness. The moon was obscured by huge, ink-black clouds. 'There's going to be one hell of a storm, I think,' he'd said quietly.

'Gotta go, Joyce,' whispered Felice, spying Prairie in the bar. She hung up the phone, a little too quickly. 'Hello Chickadee!' she said brightly. 'Whoo-wee, was it windy last night? I hardly slept a wink! Darn shutter downstairs banged away until I could stand it no more and made Arthur go down and see to it. It's a chill wind that blows no ill, that's for sure.'

'Good morning, Felice,' Prairie said quietly, inwardly rolling her eyes.

'Heavy or light breakfast today?'

'Heavy please, Felice.' Without Mabel from twelve o'clock until three o'clock, she'd be on her own in the exchange, unable to take tea breaks and limited comfort breaks. *Better have some ballast,* she thought to herself.

'Big day?' Felice queried on her way to the kitchen. Prairie was in no mind to explain Mabel Wattage's absence from the exchange. Gil was right. Small town gossip was the lifeline of a rural community. Mabel deserved privacy. So instead, she said 'No, just super-hungry for some reason.'

'Must've been all that excitement last night. I'm sure I'll never get the stench of dead sheep off the floorboards. Thank Gawd Heck didn't have a mind to dump it on the carpet! Can you imagine the stain?'

'What happened to it?' Prairie asked.

'Well, Old Johnny Whillick wanted to take it home for the pot, but on account of it being poisoned an' all we said best not. My Stanley had the presence of mind to suggest the vet should take a look at it, so he and Tom Langtree took it out the back and covered it up. Hopefully, Dr Ted can get out here later today and take the stinking thing off my hands. Bacon? Sausage?'

Prairie suddenly felt queasy. 'Actually Felice, I'll just have poached eggs on toast.'

○ ○ ○

The *Granary Caff* was no different. Prairie ducked in to grab a sandwich and something sweet for afternoon tea, and it seemed that every table was discussing Hector Johnson's dead sheep. The entire café hushed when she walked through the door. Nobody made eye contact with her.

'I'll have a ham and cheese sandwich, please Rosie,' said Prairie when she got to the counter. 'And one of those darling little butterfly cakes. Could I possibly trouble you to fill this thermos with hot coffee too?'

'Of course! Picnic today?' asked Rosie-Mandy, thumping the keys of the till.

'No, just work – I prefer your coffee though,' Prairie lied, knowing full well the great tins of instant coffee were all one and the same throughout the town.

'Dreadful scene in the pub last night,' said Rosie-Mandy quietly, as she took a five-dollar note from Prairie.

'Yes, most upsetting,' Prairie replied, pocketing her change.

'Damn salt monsters,' one patron murmured, loud enough for Prairie to hear. His wife shushed him. 'Crocodiles they are,' he said louder. 'Saltwater crocs.'

Prairie turned and recognised him as a regular patron of the Harvest Hotel. He'd been at the bar last night. Who was she kidding? The whole town had probably been in there. And those who weren't had heard about the commotion by now. She had no doubt that Olive and the Night Boy had spent their shifts connecting calls all the way from Blackwatch to Dumbogan, helping this awful news spread like a virus. Something in Prairie flamed.

'Was that for my benefit, Sir?' she said, indignant, fixing the man with a gaze of steel.

'All these blow-ins from outta town,' said another patron. 'They come here and act like they own the place. Poisoning our town and feeding off the carcass. Blowflies. Saltwater crocs and blowflies.' There was some sniggering. Other patrons just stared at her silently. Prairie eyeballed each one of them, committing their faces to memory. Then, she snatched up a saltshaker from the table. The wife gasped.

'I hope none of you use this,' she said loudly, holding it up. She wanted to hurl it against the wall and watch the glass shattered into a thousand pieces. 'Seems you are salty enough!' She slammed it down on the table in front of the man and his wife, daring them to retaliate. Nobody did. She wanted to flee the café, but she'd already paid and besides, she wasn't going to give them the satisfaction of watching her slink out. So, she stood at the counter, claiming her space in the town, with a face of granite. Rosie-Mandy smiled sympathetically and handed her a paper bag and her thermos.

'Thank you, Rosie. Good day. Good day, Simone.' For the first time ever, Simone smiled at her too. *Blow-in, indeed!* Prairie whirled about on her heel, and looking neither left nor right, strode out of the café. The café, where *her* hard-earned money helped to keep Rosie-Mandy in business. In the town, where she slept and woke in the hotel room *she* paid for. And off she went to *her* job at the local telephone exchange – to help these small-minded people spread their pestilential gossip from farm to farm. Prairie Humble was livid.

○　○　○

Baby Blue charged down Grain Street, with Prairie gripping the steering wheel like a determined charioteer and muttering curse words aloud. She may even have exceeded the speed limit and imagined what she would say to Constable Timms if he dared to pull her over. *'Go and find the real sheep killer!'* she would shout at him.

The wind had blown itself out overnight but had left behind a bank of dark clouds low on the horizon. Huge anvil-shaped thunderclouds. They matched Prairie's mood. Past *Haughty Couture* and *Battersby's Meats*, past *Carlson's Homewares, Evans & Son*, the jeweller, and *Reynolds' Auto*. She wanted to drive on and on, away from the town and its spiteful rumourmongers and out to the salt lands. Out to Gil. She wanted to be nowhere near the town, and everywhere near him.

The red lights of a stationary ambulance in the driveway of the Comfrey house caught her eye. She allowed her head to turn despite her earlier promise never to look at that house again and saw that Constable Timms would never have caught her speeding, because he was there too, in the driveway, and medics from the local Aid Post were coming out of the house with a stretcher. Agnes Comfrey was on the porch, and then the scene was gone. Baby Blue hurtled towards the exchange.

I should turn back, thought Prairie, although she wasn't entirely sure why. She looked at her watch and saw that it was five to nine. She had wasted precious moments ordering eggs she hardly ate at the hotel and arguing with locals in the café and now there were no moments to spare for Agnes Comfrey – not, she supposed, that Agnes would welcome them. Besides, Constable Timms had it all under control, hadn't he?

As the exchange came into view, she turned onto Telegraph Road and prayed that Briar would not press her about Mabel's termination. When she saw the little gravel carpark empty though, she was perplexed. Briar's red Mini Cooper should have been there, given she was supposed to start at six.

Prairie switched off the engine, collected her bag, her thermos and lunch, and crunched up the gravel path to the door. She pushed against the door and found it locked. She rang the bell and waited. Nobody answered. Prairie sighed and set her thermos and lunch on the doorstep. She trudged through the little garden bed to peer through the front window, but it was too high to get a good look inside. She rapped on the windowpane and waited. When nobody came, she walked around the perimeter of the building.

'Briar!' she called. '*Briar!* Are you in there?' There was no answer. *How odd,* thought Prairie. *Oh!* Panic suddenly gripped her. *What if someone has broken in and tied her up? Or maybe she's unconscious? Oh dear!*

Prairie's heart began to pound. It didn't make sense. Where was Briar's car? And where was the Night Boy? She would have to drive back to town and summons help. If she could find Olive, they could come back with Olive's key. She was just about to get into Baby Blue when Constable Timms' patrol car rolled down Telegraph Road and into the gravel drive, pulling in behind the Morris Minor. Prairie was relieved to see him.

'Oh, Constable Timms!' she gushed. 'I'm so glad you're here. Something's wrong!'

'Yes, Miss Humble, it is,' he said, alighting from the vehicle. 'I need you to put a call through to Golga for me. I'm afraid it's the Widow Comfrey.'

'What?' said Prairie. 'No. I mean, oh gosh, of course yes. But I can't. I can't get into the exchange,' she explained. 'What's happened to Mrs Comfrey?'

'What do you mean you can't get in?' Timms stared at her blankly. 'Who's in there?'

'Well, nobody seems to be in there. At least, the door is locked, and nobody is answering the bell. I've banged on the windows too and called out.'

'Who's supposed to be on duty?' he asked, incredulous.

'Briar Lee was supposed to start at six this morning.'

'Don't you have a key?' Timms asked.

Prairie shook her head. 'None of us have keys except Olive Wellshorn and Mr Peterson.'

Timms sighed. 'Well, that is incredibly inconvenient. I need to call the Coroner in Golga. This explains why Miss Comfrey couldn't get through to the Aid Post.'

'What's happened?' asked Prairie.

'I'm afraid Gwinny Comfrey has had rather a nasty fall.'

'Oh dear. Will she be alright?'

'I doubt it, Miss Humble,' said Constable Timms. 'She's dead.'

9
The Missing Telephonist

'**P**oor Agnes,' said Prairie, as they drove along towards Wheatsheaf. 'She must be so terribly upset.' The first drops of rain had begun to fall.

'Yes,' said Timms, switching the windscreen wipers on. 'She was beside herself. Barely coherent when she got to the police station. She couldn't call for the ambulance, you see.'

'What happened?' asked Prairie.

'Gwinny Comfrey is not terribly steady on her feet. Agnes says she wanted a book from a shelf she couldn't reach. Agnes was busy and asked her to wait, but it seems old Gwinny got impatient and climbed on a chair to get the book herself. She never did have much in the way of patience. Made a right old mess in the living room. Brought the whole bookshelf down on top of herself.'

'Oh, my goodness,' Prairie gasped. 'Where is Agnes now? Does she have anyone to help her?'

'I stopped at the church before coming here and asked Father Childers to sit with her until I get back. Of all days for Miss Lee to be tardy.'

'She's not just tardy, Constable – she was supposed to be there at six o'clock. It's now nine forty-five. I'm worried something has happened to her. And possibly the Night Boy. He should have been waiting until someone arrived to relieve him.'

'Call me *Emmanuel*,' he said. 'Unless, of course, you need to speak to me in an official capacity.'

'Of course,' said Prairie, and folded her hands in her lap. She would never call him *Emmanuel*, she was sure. A peal of thunder rolled overhead.

Timms drove straight to the home of Olive Wellshorn. It took some minutes for Olive to answer the knock, and she was surprised to find Prairie and the local constabulary on her doorstep.

'Prairie? Constable Timms? Whatever's the matter?'

'We've come for the keys to the exchange, Miss Wellshorn. I'm afraid Miss Humble is locked out, and I need to contact Golga as a matter of some urgency.'

'Where's Briar?' Olive asked. 'Please, come in while I fetch the keys.'

'Briar's not there, Olive,' said Prairie. 'Who was supposed to be on the crypt shift?'

'Tom Rizzoli. Has he not seen Briar at all?'

'I don't know,' said Prairie. 'There's no sign of him there either!'

'Oh, my goodness,' said Olive, grabbing her bag and pulling on a pair of green pumps. 'We'd better swing by the Rizzoli house first, Constable Timms.'

○　○　○

Tom Rizzoli was surly. Prairie had never met him before and was not sure whether he was annoyed at being roused from his bed so soon after climbing into it, or whether this was his natural character.

'What time did you leave the exchange, Tom?' asked Olive.

'Ten past six this morning,' Tom answered bluntly.

'You didn't wait for Briar?'

'No,' he sneered. 'I'm sick to death of waiting on her. We all are. She's not been on time for one shift that I can remember. She's got a damn nerve snitching on me.'

'She didn't snitch on you, Tom. We haven't seen her. How did you think she'd get in? You know we can't leave the lines abandoned,' Olive scolded gently.

'They're not abandoned. I switched through to Blackwatch before I left. I was sure she'd be along soon enough. I'm fed up with her eating into my time. I thought she probably had a sneaky key or something.'

'Why would you think that?' asked Olive. Tom shrugged.

'Are you sure you switched them through properly?' Timms asked. 'We have a report of a resident being unable to contact the Community Aid Post earlier this morning.'

Tom shrugged again. 'Not my fault. Maybe there's something wrong with the line. Maybe a pole went down in the storm last night. I definitely switched 'em through.'

Turning away from the Rizzoli house, Olive was concerned. 'We should go to Briar's house, Constable. She may be hurt or ill. Could you check on her? Prairie and I should really get to the exchange and retrieve our lines from Blackwatch. Mr Peterson will be apoplectic when he finds out.'

'I really need to call the coroner....'

'Fine – I'll go. Prairie, take my keys. You know how to retrieve the lines?'

'I'll work it out,' said Prairie, taking the key ring.

Olive gave a grateful smile. 'I'll be along as soon as I can.'

O   O   O

It was raining harder now. Prairie put the key in the exchange door and let them in. The little room still held some of the heat from the radiator. There was no sign of Briar Lee. Prairie noticed that her coffee mug, a fine white China piece adorned with roses, lay untouched on the kitchen draining board. She saw an illuminated red light on the panel and the jack in the portal for the exchange at Blackwatch. Prairie picked up her headset, dialled the exchange in the little town to the east and requested the lines be directed back to Wheatsheaf.

'What's happened?' asked the telephonist on the other end of the line. Prairie didn't know what to say.

'Unexpected illness,' she lied. 'So sorry to have patched through for so long.'

Next, she dialled the coroner's office in Golga and motioned for Constable Timms to pick up a headset. 'Putting you through now,' she whispered. Timms looked uncomfortable. Prairie gathered he'd prefer not to speak to the coroner in front of her, but there was nowhere else for her to go. She had to stay at her post.

'It's Constable Emmanuel Timms from Wheatsheaf, Sir. I'm afraid I need to report a deceased person…Guinevere Comfrey, female…eighty-five. Mode of death….' He looked across at Prairie, removed his headset briefly and said, 'I apologise Miss Humble, this may be quite grim.'

'That's fine, Constable. I'm not listening.'

'Mode of death seems to be a fall. She appears to have been standing on a foot stool when she fell. She's…clutched at the bookshelf on her way down. Brought it crashing down on top of her… Yes, the local ambulance driver helped me move the bookshelf… She's been transported to the morgue at Golga Base Hosp –'

Prairie heard a raised voice on the other end of the line and Constable Timms reddened. 'Oh! I'm so frightfully sorry, I didn't realise. Of course, yes. Of course, we shouldn't have moved her – I see that now. You're quite right, Sir. Only…well her daughter lives there and I didn't like to leave…Yes, Sir. Yes, Sir. Of course. My apologies again.' He hung up. Prairie fiddled intently with the range of jacks and buttons on her switchboard and pretended to be unaware of the young officer's discomfort.

'Apparently we shouldn't have moved the…Mrs Comfrey,' he said. 'I didn't consider it a suspicious death. Seemed pretty straight forward to me. I thought you only left them – I mean the *deceased person* – in situ, when the death was suspicious. Oh well, I suppose that's my Senior Constable position on hold for another twelve months.' He attempted a smile, but Prairie could see how dejected he was.

'I shouldn't think you'd have to deal with too many deaths in Wheatsheaf,' she said gently. 'Don't be hard on yourself. You could hardly leave poor Mrs Comfrey under a bookcase. What if she'd been alive?'

'Quite,' he said. 'Well, I'd better be getting back to the Comfrey residence. I hope Miss Lee turns up safe and sound.' He stood up, walked to the door and then turned back. 'Thank you, Miss Humble.'

'Whatever for?' asked Prairie.

'For your…kindness. It is…appreciated. Perhaps we could have a drink one….'

The switchboard lit up. 'Wheatsheaf. Number please?' Prairie held up her hands in apology.

'Yes, of course,' Constable Timms waved goodbye and hastily let himself out.

Saved by the switch, thought Prairie.

O   O   O

An hour later, someone knocked at the exchange door. *I hope that's not Constable Timms again*, thought Prairie, rising to answer it. Olive pushed her way in and hung up her coat.

'How did you go?' Prairie asked.

Olive shook her head. 'No sign of her. She rents the little flat above the Post Office. I got Paula McInerney to let me in – she has a spare key. I thought Briar might be in there ill, but it doesn't even look as though her bed has been slept in. Tell you what though, she has more clothes in her closet than are on the racks in *Haughty Couture!* And the shoes and handbags! She's not done a runner, at least, not that I could tell – although her Mini's not parked in the street. I wonder where she is. God, I need a cuppa. Want one?'

'Yes please.' Prairie had left her thermos in Constable Timms' patrol car along with her lunch.

'We should report her missing, I suppose?' Olive called from the tearoom. Prairie heard her putting the kettle on, the teaspoon clinking in a coffee cup.

'Well, she was with us in the pub when Heck Johnson brought his dead sheep in…that wasn't long after you left. Maybe six-thirty? I think Gil and I went upstairs before she left….'

'Oh, did you?' Olive whipped her head around the door frame.

'To the balcony. Gil was very upset. It was awful the way Heck Johnson turned on him, just because he works for Blush Salt. We said goodnight at about seven o'clock, thank you very much, and I am pleased to report I spent the night alone in my bed.'

Olive came through with two cups of coffee and put one down in front of Prairie. Prairie noticed it was Briar's cup. Olive saw her hesitation and said, 'I didn't even think. Here, I'll tip it into another.'

'No, that's okay,' said Prairie. 'I'm sure Briar won't mind. Wherever she is.'

Olive sipped her coffee thoughtfully. The switch lit up and Prairie put the call through. It was Dr Ted, the veterinarian, wanting the Johnson farm. Prairie thought about Gil again and wondered how he was.

'Where do you suppose Briar has gone?' she asked Olive.

Olive shrugged. 'Beats the hell outta me. I mean, I know she can be a little unreliable at times. Yes, she is often late for her shifts – Tommy had a point there – but she's never let me down before. She's hardly missed a shift in three years and she always, *always* lets me know if she can't make it.'

'How long have you known Briar?'

'Three years?' Olive answered, thinking. Prairie was surprised.

'Is she not from Wheatsheaf?'

'Oh, yes. But I'm not. I came here from Golga about three and a half years ago.'

'Really?' said Prairie. Olive nodded.

'Yep. I sat my telephonist exam up there, but I've worked all around. Did a lot of temping, just like you. I did a stretch out in Broken Hill – loved the place, and one in Kalgoorlie. *That* was eye-opening.'

Prairie's eyes widened. 'I'll bet!' she said. 'I've always wanted to go to West Wyalong – I'm in love with Russell Drysdale paintings.'

'You still can,' said Olive. 'I tell you, it's something else out there in Kalgoorlie. Talk about the Wild West! Anyway, I came out here as an auditor from the Golga post and Mr Peterson offered me a senior position. I really liked the town, so I accepted.'

'Do you think you'll stay?'

Olive nodded as she drank her coffee. 'For the time being. I feel like I'm part of the furniture now.'

'And Briar?'

'Briar started as a telephonist here just after I took up the senior position. She's a local girl originally, but I know she spent a good deal of time away. Her folks moved to Golga when she was about sixteen. They stayed up there as far as I know, but some-thing brought her back. I'm not sure what – she never seems to have anything good to say about Wheatsheaf and she's off shop-ping in Golga at every given opportunity. I've often said to her that we could put in a good word at the exchange up there – although I'm not sure Mr Peterson would agree. He spends more time up there than anywhere and I wouldn't say he's Briar's biggest fan.'

'No? Why's that then?'

'She gives him a terrible amount of cheek. She's young and full of pizazz. Her very presence irritates him. You can see it writ-ten all over his face when she breezes in. If Mr Peterson had his way, I'm sure we'd all be tied to a stove by our apron-strings.'

Prairie laughed. 'He's no suffragette,' she observed.

'Oh, my word no. Very traditional is our Mr Peterson. I know I must confuse him. He can't work out why I'm not married with a tribe of children, but he's not game to ask me. And, as I say, Briar was a little tardy. Mr Peterson's big on timekeeping. Well, we have to be in our job, don't we? Oh, that reminds me – were the phones patched through to Blackwatch like Tommy said?'

Prairie nodded. 'Oh yes, they were just fine.'

'Thank goodness for that,' Olive sighed. 'That's one less drama to sort out. I'd better ring Peterson and tell him what's happened. He'll be livid. When she does turn up, I hope she's got a damn good excuse. He's fired Mabel so I doubt he'll think twice about giving Briar her marching orders.'

'Olive,' Prairie asked quietly. 'Do you know why Mr Peterson let Mabel go?'

Olive took a deep breath. 'Yes,' she said flatly. 'Do you?'

Prairie nodded. 'Yes. Mabel told me.'

Olive's face softened. 'Shame,' she said quietly. 'Damn shame. We're governed by the wrong kind of morality here.' She shook her head, put on her headset and dialled the exchange at Golga to ask for Fidel Peterson.

10

Passionfruit Sponge

At the junction of Telegraph Road with the highway, Prairie stopped Baby Blue and deliberated. The wind whipped down the road and buffeted the car. The sky, pregnant with granite-coloured clouds, wanted to birth a deluge but seemed to be having trouble. Rain fell sporadically in big, constipated drops. Prairie's watch told her it was ten past three. She supposed Gil would still be at the saltworks. She longed to pay him a visit, to see how he was, but knew he could be anywhere around the vast lake. Besides, she didn't wish to draw any unwelcome attention for him, so she indicated right and followed a passing road-train from the north, down into Wheatsheaf. She slowed as she passed the Comfrey homestead, out of respect for the dead and curiosity, in equal measure.

Constable Timms' patrol car was gone. She expected Olive would be paying him a visit at the station later. They had agreed with Mr Peterson that if Briar Lee had not made contact by six o'clock that night, the constabulary would be contacted. The police would not consider filing a Missing Person's Report if the missing had not been missed for more than twenty-four hours. Although Fidel Peterson did not miss her at all, he conceded that disappearing for a whole day was out of character even for the irksome and unreliable Briar Lee, and agreed that something should be done about it.

Without thinking it through, Prairie swung Baby Blue into the Comfrey's driveway. The archway of trees ushered her in, swaying back and forth. With a blue scarf tied over her head to keep her hair in place, Prairie mounted the steps to the porch and rang the bell. Moments passed and Prairie was about to turn away when Agnes Comfrey answered. She was hollow-eyed and her hair had been pulled back into a messy bun. She looked, understandably, as though she had not slept for days. She wore an apron printed with faded yellow daisies over a dull grey housedress.

'I'm so sorry to hear about your mother, Miss Comfrey,' Prairie gushed before she could be sent away. 'I know I have no business being here, but I just wanted to pay my respects to you and…see whether there was anything I could do to help?'

Agnes Comfrey regarded her for a few moments. Then her face collapsed in on itself, tired of bearing a terrible weight. She held the door open wide. 'Please, come in.'

Prairie stepped into the dim hallway. Dark-panelled skirting ran along the base of the walls and the floorboards were bare save for a heavy crimson rug. The house smelled faintly musty, as though it had been closed up for some time.

'Please excuse the mess, Miss Humble. I'm afraid I've rather a lot to clear up.'

'Please don't worry on my account, Miss Comfrey.'

'Would you like some tea? I don't have much in the way of anything else to offer you.'

'Please don't go to any trouble….'

'It's no trouble.'

'Then thank you. Tea would be lovely.'

'How do you take it?'

'White – with one, please.'

Agnes Comfrey left Prairie in the living room while she busied herself in the kitchen. Prairie sat down on a leather sofa and sunk further than she expected to. She looked around. She could see where the heavy bookcase had been righted. Books and framed photographs had been hastily shoved back into place. Some were upside down.

On the floor, were remnants of the affray; some pottery shards and a smattering of dirt, presumably from a broken plant pot. Prairie stared at the spot and tried to imagine Gwinny Comfrey, lifeless beneath a mound of books and pictures. She shuddered and pulled her gaze from the floor. Her eyes darted about the austere room. The walls were a drab beige, like buttery, milky coffee. Prairie could not tell whether the colour was intentional, or the yellowing of age. A black Bakelite telephone sat on a stand in the corner.

Agnes returned with a tray and handed Prairie a cup on a saucer. The cup was crafted of delicate, fine bone China and covered in blue forget-me-nots. Prairie guessed it was decades old. Agnes sat upright in a wing-back chair opposite her.

'I…I want to thank you for your kindness the other day, Miss Humble.'

'Please, call me Prairie.'

'Prairie. That's such a pretty name. It was very kind of you to think of Mother and me. I'm sorry she was so…so rude. She can be…could be…difficult, with strangers.' She sipped her tea hurriedly to cover her embarrassment.

'I understand completely,' said Prairie. 'It seems strangers are not well-liked in Wheatsheaf. I was called a *blow-in blowfly* yesterday by a gentleman in the café – I use the term *gentleman* loosely, of course.'

Agnes shook her head. 'I apologise on behalf of our town,' she said. 'That was most ungracious. But believe me, you could live here all your life and still not be accepted by some of the townsfolk. Some people are so very quick to judge. It's fear, I think, that makes them vile at times. They don't like things that are…different.' She sighed and put the cup back on its saucer.

'Have you lived in Wheatsheaf all your life, Miss Comfrey?'

'Agnes, please. Yes. Born and bred. In this very house. I don't really know much of life except these walls and Grain Street. I'm told there is a wide world above the dinner plate, though I know very little of it.'

'You have ever such a beautiful lake just down the road,' said Prairie, thinking about Gil once again.

'Yes, I have seen it once or twice. But not for a while. Mother doesn't…Mother *didn't* much like it. She said it stank of the sea. Rotting fish and seaweed. And the seagulls and flies annoyed her.' Her hands trembled and rattled the cup on the saucer. She set them down on the table and rubbed her hands together.

'Well, you must come with me one time,' said Prairie. 'I love to sit there sketching.'

'Sketching?'

'Yes,' said Prairie. 'I like to draw things. Sometimes, I like to paint over my pencil sketches with water-colour paints. I'm not terribly good, but I do enjoy it. I find it soothing.'

Agnes nodded. 'I crochet.' She patted a chequered blanket, draped over the arm of the chair. 'This is one of mine,' she said. 'Took me most of last Winter. I like to do one a season.'

Prairie smiled. 'It's beautiful,' she said, admiring the black, white and grey chequered pattern. It matched the sky today perfectly. 'Miss…Agnes. Is there anything I can do to help you? This must be such a distressing time for you.'

'Thank you, Miss…Prairie. But I need to be alone with my thoughts just now. The place needs a good clear out. It will help me take my mind off Mother. I thought I might even paint the walls. Blue. With white trim. I like sky blue. Don't you?'

'Oh yes,' said Prairie. 'Very much. Blue is my favourite colour.' She looked at the telephone. 'May I use your phone briefly?'

'Of course. If it's working. I had trouble earlier.'

Prairie stood up and crossed to the stand. She picked up the phone, tapped the receiver twice and waited for the dial tone. She then dialled the exchange. Olive answered.

'Wheatsheaf. Number please?'

'Oh Olive, it's Prairie.'

'You're calling from the Comfrey place?'

'Yessss...any sign of Briar?'

'None. I'll be going straight to Constable Timms when Ingrid gets here.' Prairie replaced the heavy handset back in its cradle.

'I never will understand technology,' said Agnes, shaking her head. 'Sometimes it works, sometimes it doesn't.'

'You're probably not on the main line out here. It's not uncommon to get crossed wires with these party lines. Thank you for the tea, Agnes. I should be getting back to town. Are you sure there's nothing I can do to help you?'

'Thank you, Prairie. I appreciate you stopping by.'

On her way to the door, Prairie crossed the spot where Gwinny Comfrey had died. She bent and picked up the pottery shards. 'I'd hate you to cut your feet on these,' she said.

Agnes walked her to the door, bid her goodbye and shut it behind her. Seeing the dustbin at the side of the house, Prairie opened the lid to toss the pottery shards in. The remains of a yellow passionfruit sponge stared up at her, smashed to pieces like the pottery shards.

Death: Part 3

Felice rang the brass bell behind the bar. 'Thunderstorm warning, folks! Batter up your hatches!'

'Oh dear,' said Prairie, a piece of steak pie midway to her lips. 'Not another chill wind blowing no ill.' She winked at Gil, hoping to cheer him up. Her attempts were in vain. Gil Sanders was miserable. Every time the bar door opened, he turned to see who was coming in.

'That's all we need,' he said, missing the joke.

'I'm sure it was just a nasty coincidence,' she said.

'It's a nasty scratch, is what it is. And *two* punctured tyres? That's some coincidence alright.' He stabbed a chip with his fork. 'The accountants have gone back to Golga early. They're commuting down for the rest of the week. Two hours each way! That's not sustainable,' he said and stabbed another chip. Prairie regarded him. He was pale; dark circles beneath his eyes made him look sullen. At least out at the salt works, behind its security fence, the locals couldn't get to him there.

'Prairie,' he said eventually, 'I'm not sure how much longer I can stay here.'

'But you haven't done anything wrong, Gil. Why should you go away?'

'Every time I walk into the bar, the café, the grocer's – people stop talking and stare at me. Then they murmur under their breath things they want me to hear. And now my car! What next?'

Prairie finished chewing and swallowed. She didn't know. She glanced at her watch and saw that it was six o'clock. With no news of Briar Lee, Olive would be on her way to the police station.

○ ○ ○

It was dark on the road for early evening in Autumn. The sky was a mass of black clouds. Fat drops of rain splatted against the windshield of Sam Swallow's rig as he cut a swathe through the wind. *Pock! Pock! Pock!* Ten wheels whooshed along the tarmac sending spray behind him in a great fan across the road. The beams of his headlights illuminated the sliver of road before him. The familiar outline of Wheatsheaf's great silo appeared in the centre of the road. Not far. He wiped an eye, red and watery with fatigue. The haul between Golden Grain's silos dotted all about the countryside sometimes meant the best part of the day behind the wheel of his truck. But that was during the harvest. He was on his way home now, and he let his mind wander to the big, amber pint he was going to have Felice pour him when he got to the hotel.

Up ahead, through the curtain of rain, the headlights illuminated something in the road. Was it a roo? He slammed on the brakes and the heavy truck skidded to a halt. He felt a sickening thud as something went under the wheels. Shaken, Sam looked in his wing mirror but could see nothing in the darkness behind him. He climbed out of his cab, in the pouring rain and retraced the steps to the back of his truck.

'Oh, dear God! Mercy!' he cried. He looked up and down the pitch-black highway, whimpering. Then, he sloshed back to the cab, climbed in and drove his rig faster than was sensible into Wheatsheaf.

Bronzed, leathery men from the fields lined the bar. Some slouched, loudly 'shooting the breeze' after a long day. Others huddled, murmuring in concerned tones about the weather. The words *'damn nerve showing his face in here'* cut through the din and reached the ears of Prairie and Gil. They looked up to see two men, leaning lazily at the bar. One hadn't even bothered to remove his hat; such was his haste to quench his thirst. He absent-mindedly twirled his half-empty pint glass, the golden liquid sloshing about inside, as he stared straight at them. Gil bristled. Prairie laid a hand on his arm. 'Just ignore him,' she said.

'You got some nerve, Salt Man,' the barfly said, louder.

'I've had enough of this,' said Gil and pushed back his chair. At full height, Gil stood at six feet, two inches. He was muscular and fit. But Prairie doubted he'd be a match for the two earth-hardened men at the bar.

'Gil, please. Let's just go.'

'I think this man has something to say first,' he said, glaring at the farmer. 'Come on then pal, what is it?'

'Okay ladies, handbags away,' said Arthur, moving towards them along the bar. 'If there's blood to be shed it won't be on my bloody floor, so fuck off outside if you want to belt each other.'

'Wallopers!' called a cockatoo from the front of the pub, as the door swung open, and Constable Timms strode in. Olive was right behind him. The crowd that had begun to swell around the men receded, like an ebbing tide. The farmers returned to their drink.

'I've had a gutful today, Prairie,' said Gil, irritably. 'I'll see you tomorrow.'

'Please Gil, just wait —'

'Prairie!' called Olive, as she and Constable Timms made their way to her table. Gil turned and went upstairs.

'Is there any word on Briar?' Prairie asked.

'No,' said Olive, shaking her head.

'Miss Humble, would you mind coming to the police station with us? I need to file an official Missing Persons' Report. You may have been the last person to see Miss Lee.'

'What?' said Prairie. 'Me?'

'She was still here with you when I left for the exchange, wasn't she?' said Olive. 'You said she was here, just before Heck Johnson's sheep made an appearance?'

'Yes,' said Prairie. 'Yes, that's right.' She bent to collect her scarf and purse.

The hotel door crashed open with the force of the wind behind it and Sam Swallow burst into the bar, dripping and incoherent.

'I've killed her!' he cried. 'I didn't mean to. She was just there, in the rain! Oh god!'

'Get the man a brandy,' Arthur bellowed to his son. Stan held a glass up to the optic and passed it to Sam. Sam swallowed the contents in one gulp and sobbed.

'What on earth is the matter?' Constable Timms demanded.

'Oh Constable Timms! I think I killed her. I didn't mean to. She was just there.'

'Who was? Where?'

'The silo. She went under the wheels of my truck. Oh god…' He pressed his hands to his face. Constable Timms eyes widened, and he grabbed the glass from Sam before he could accept another shot of brandy.

'Have you been drinking at the wheel again?' he asked sharply.

'Just this,' said Sam. 'Oh sweet Jesus. It was awful.'

'You'd better come with me,' said Constable Timms.

'Please don't make me go back there.'

'Grow up, man,' the constable growled. 'You have to show me where she is.'

'Who is it?' asked Olive, but Sam just shook his head and sobbed uncontrollably. Prairie and Olive exchanged worried glances.

'Arthur, will you or Stan come with me?' Timms asked. 'I might need help. I'll get none from him.'

'I'll go,' said Stan, throwing down a tea-towel.

'I'll come too,' said Prairie.

'No thank you, Miss Humble. This is no place for a…'

'For a what?' said Prairie flatly. She tied her scarf around her head resolutely.

'I'm coming too,' said Olive. She and Prairie followed the men out into the rain.

The five of them piled into Timms' patrol car and drove, grim-faced, out to the silo. The only sounds were the rhythmic beating of the wipers against the windshield and the *slooosh* of rain as the tyres slicked water from the road. And the muffled sobs of Sam Swallow.

○   ○   ○

The silo loomed in the darkness before them, cold and sentinel. Prairie shivered. Constable Timms slowed the patrol car.

'Is she there?' asked Sam, wedged in the back seat between Prairie and Olive. The patrol car crept along the road until in the beam of the headlights, something on the side of the road caught Stan's eye.

'Over there, to the left,' he said. Prairie, behind Stan, strained to see out of the window. Timms pulled the car onto the shoulder and left the engine running, directing the headlights towards a crumpled form by the side of the road.

'She wasn't there when I hit her. She was in the middle of the road, but she went sideways a bit.' He held his hands to his face. 'I couldn't brake in time. Please don't make me get out and look,' he said.

Prairie felt queasy but opened the car door. 'Miss Humble,' said the policeman. 'I think it would be best if you and Miss Wellshorn stay here with Sam. Just until…well, no point in us all upsetting ourselves, is there?' Prairie glanced at Olive, who nodded. She was as white as Sam Swallow. Prairie pulled the door shut to keep out the rain and the three of them sat silently in the back of the patrol car while Constable Timms and Stan Banbury got out to inspect the crumpled, lifeless form. The rain had eased up a little, but the land was thoroughly soaked. Sam Swallow put his head in his hands and sobbed quietly.

'I didn't mean to kill her,' he said. 'She was just there! I thought she was a kangaroo.' Prairie patted his back soothingly.

'It's alright Sam,' she said. 'You weren't to know.'

The men stood over the body. Constable Timms waved his torch and shook his head. He returned to the car, grim-faced and opened the boot, from which he retrieved a heavy white sheet. He opened the car door and leaned in.

'I'm sorry to say this, but it appears to be Miss Lee.'

'Oh Briar,' Olive gasped and clasped her hands to her mouth.

'She's deceased. It's an awful thing to ask, ladies, and I'm sorry to do it, but could one of you please positively identify her, for the record?'

Sam Swallow let out a great racking sob. Prairie glanced at Olive, but Olive shook her head.

'I don't think I can.' She looked about to faint.

'I'll go,' said Prairie, and opened the car door again. The rain stuck to her lashes and bejewelled her headscarf. She set her jaw firmly and followed Constable Timms. He draped the sheet over the body to hide the worst of the damage. Prairie looked down on a sodden figure. Blonde hair, made dark by the rain, streaked in writhing tendrils across the face.

Oh Briar, thought Prairie sadly. *What has happened to you?* She took a deep breath and squatted down beside the lifeless mound.

'May I?' she asked Constable Timms. He nodded and directed the beam of his torch to assist. Prairie gently smoothed back the dank wet hair. There was no mistaking the fine features of Briar Lee. The delicate, upturned nose, the full lips, usually blood red, now blue. Then Prairie noticed something else and recoiled, snatching her hand away.

'Oh, good God!' she gasped.

Briar Lee's throat had been slit.

O O O

16

Broken Wires

Prairie turned away and took a great gulp of air. *I will not be sick,* she told herself. Stan Banbury backed away a little, but Constable Timms squatted down beside the corpse.

'Good God, Miss Humble, you're right,' he said. He placed the sheet over the mottled face of Briar Lee. They went back to the patrol car. 'Sam, could you please tell me exactly where in the road you hit Miss Lee?'

'I swear I didn't mean to kill her….'

'It's alright, Sam,' said the constable. 'It looks like she may have already been dead when you hit her.' A look of disbelief and then relief flooded the face of Sam Swallow. Olive stared at Prairie aghast. Sam got out of the patrol car and led the constable to the spot in the road where he thought the impact occurred.

'I come level with the haul road,' he said, looking to the right, 'And then I seen a figure in the road…I thought it was a roo. It must've been about here. Yeah, look, you can see in the wet where my brakes locked up and I skidded. I hit her and she flew over there aways, where she is now.'

Timms shone his light over the patch of road, noting the skid marks. 'There's no blood I can see,' he said. 'The rain would have washed it away by now.'

'Surely she wasn't killed in the middle of the road?' said Prairie. 'A slit throat would produce a lot of blood, but I can't imagine someone standing in the middle of the road to do it, can you?'

Timms stiffened. Sam looked ill. 'Can I go back into the car now, Officer Timms? I don't feel so good.'

'Of course, Sam.'

Sam tottered back to the patrol car, doing his best not to look at the white mound on the side of the road.

'Perhaps she was killed nearby,' said Prairie, looking up at the dark silo. Timms craned his neck. Wheatsheaf's house of grain could have been one of any number, dotted all over the countryside. It sat between the train tracks and the road, the tracks bisecting the road not far from where Baby Blue had almost collided with Sam Swallow's truck. There were twin concrete cylindrical towers next to a shorter rotund structure made of tin, and a long building with a steepled roof.

'I doubt we'll find anything useful now,' said Timms. 'It's too dark and wet. We need to get the body…I mean, Miss Lee…off the road. It's so undignified to leave her out here.'

Prairie agreed but reminded Constable Timms of his earlier reprimand by the coroner. 'You don't want to be told off again,' she said quietly.

'That's a good point,' Timms conceded. 'Perhaps I'd best ring Head Quarters at Golga for direction. Come on, I'll take you all back to town.'

'We can't just leave Briar here,' said Prairie. 'What if somebody drives by and stops to investigate?'

'Another good point,' said Timms, thinking hard.

'What if you were to take Olive, Stan and Sam back to town, and I stay here? Olive and Sam look terrible. They're in shock. They need to get warm and dry. You can ring Golga, and then come straight back?'

'Oh no,' said Timms shaking his head. 'I can't possibly leave you out here alone, Miss Humble.'

'Yes, you can,' said Prairie. 'I'm a big girl. Look, I'll wait over there, just under the eaves of that little building. I won't move unless I absolutely have to.'

'But Miss Humble, it looks as though somebody has quite possibly *murdered* Miss Lee.' He whispered the word *'murdered.'*

'Undoubtedly, Constable,' she whispered back. 'I'm sure she didn't inflict that injury upon herself.'

'The murderer could still be in the vicinity,' said Timms quietly, casting his flashlight about furtively.

'Briar may not have been killed here. She could have been murdered elsewhere, and her body just dumped in the middle of the road. Please Constable, just leave me your torch. Get the others back into the warmth of the pub and call Golga. Please – and hurry back.'

Timms sighed and relented. There was not much else that could be done under the circumstances. Reluctantly, he followed Sam Swallow to the patrol car.

◑　◑　◑

It was cold. Prairie hugged her arms and marched on the spot in the shadows of the silo as she watched the taillights of the patrol car fade. Once they had gone altogether, she was aware just how heavy the darkness weighed. The rain had stopped, but clouds still cloaked the sky. There was occasional illumination by far-off lightning. There were no stars, no moon and no streetlights along this stretch of highway. There were corners of the silo that were as black as pitch. Prairie caught her breath with every noise. She stopped pacing and strained to listen.

Was that a door creaking open somewhere? No, just the wind drawing breath, preparing to exhale again. *Perhaps I was too hasty to send them away,* she thought. Her mind turned to Gil. *I wish he was here.* She stared across the haul road, across the highway to the spot where she could just make out the lifeless white mound. *Oh Briar. What happened to you?* she thought. *What have you done?* Prairie stiffened. *Why did I think that? How could this possibly be your fault?*

Alone in the void of the wheatfield, Prairie switched on Constable Timms' torch for company and let the beam play into the dark recesses about her. She stood under the eaves of the long, triangular grain store. Opposite her was a small square building at the foot of the two cylindrical silos. These enormous grain bins were linked by a tall rectangular structure, which Prairie supposed was a grain elevator.

She shone the torch on her watch. It had been about twenty minutes since Timms left. It felt like an hour. She hoped fervently he'd be on his way back soon. She was about to return to the roadside to wait when she heard the noise again. She stiffened. It was a faint banging, like a door had closed somewhere – softly, but loud enough to be heard in the suffocating darkness. The hairs on the nape of her neck stood to attention. The prickly sensation of gooseflesh spread across her arms and thighs. A heaviness settled itself in the pit of her stomach. She looked down the road, willing the lights of the patrol car to reappear in the darkness.

Bang!

Prairie jumped and whimpered involuntarily. *Get a hold of yourself, girl!* she chided. *A fine detective you'd make.* She swallowed the lump in her throat and flashed the beam in the direction of the noise.

'Hello?' she called uncertainly. Predictably, nobody answered and for this she was grateful. She walked quietly between the buildings towards the direction of the sound, stopping every few steps to listen. A breeze whirled about her as something creaked to her right. Prairie whipped the light of the torch around and saw a door to the outbuilding, just beneath one of the mighty cylindrical towers. It moved ever so slightly, slowly back and slowly forth on rusted hinges, groaning quietly as it went. Was this the source of the mysterious banging, she asked herself? Quietly, with beam at the ready, Prairie reached out a hand and pulled the door open.

As she did, there was a furious hiss. The beam reflected two green orbs, something inside fell and a black object shot out of the door. Prairie reeled backwards, startled, letting out a squeal as she did.

'Oh, my Lord,' she cried, starting to laugh as she recovered from the shock of having startled a feral cat. Her heart was thudding, and she bent double, laughing with relief. She pulled the door wide open and shone the light inside, making sure she would not disturb anything else. The interior was covered in dust and was empty, except for a few jerrycans and paint tins, two of which the cat had knocked over. Prairie pushed the door shut hard.

Up the road, blue flashing lights raced towards her. The headlights of another vehicle followed. There were no sirens. There was no need. With relief, Prairie hurried back to the side of the road where Constable Timms had left her.

The patrol car stopped in the middle of the highway. The other vehicle Prairie now saw was a truck belonging to *Battersby's Meats*. Constable Timms got out and rushed towards her.

'I'm sorry to have kept you, Miss Humble. I was as quick as I could be.'

'Please, Constable Timms. Call me Prairie.'

'Are you alright? You must be so cold. Here,' he said, opening the back door of the patrol car. 'Sit inside. It'll be much warmer.'

'I'm alright,' she said. 'Is that the butcher?' The truck driver strode towards them.

'Yes. Prairie, this is Phillip Rafferty. Phil, Miss Prairie Humble.' Phillip Rafferty took off his hat and bowed his head. 'I'm afraid we have some more bad news in Wheatsheaf,' Timms continued. 'Miss Wellshorn tried to put a call through to Golga, but there's no connection. It seems some wires have come down in the wind.'

'Oh dear,' said Prairie. 'I bet that will be the group on Brewer's Hill. Olive was saying those telegraph poles are notoriously in need of replacement.'

Timms nodded. 'If it's not one falling over in a stiff breeze, it's another getting struck by lightning. Brewer's Hill has a weather pattern unto itself. What that means though is that I can't get hold of the Golga Regional Headquarters or the coroner. I don't know what's best to do, given my admonishment from Mr Jacowiesz, but I can't leave Miss Lee here by the side of the road.'

'If we drove to Golga, we could be there in a couple of hours? We could fetch someone and bring them back?'

Timms nodded. 'Yes, I've thought of that. Stan Banbury is already on his way. I thought we could put Miss Lee in the refrigerated truck for the time-being. And I brought my camera to take some photographs of the scene, although I don't know that I'll capture much in the dark.'

'How is Sam?'

'Very upset, understandably. He's had a nasty shock. I've left him in the care of Felice Banbury with instructions that he's not to move his truck. No doubt the coroner will want to examine that too.'

'No doubt,' Prairie agreed.

'Can we get this over with?' asked Phil Rafferty. 'I need the truck for deliveries at dawn.'

'Oh, of course! Miss Humble – Prairie, why don't you wait here while Phil and I take care of Miss Lee?'

Prairie watched from the window of the patrol car as Constable Timms pulled back the shroud covering the young telephonist and set to work taking photographs with a box-shaped camera, on top of which was an enormous flash, like the ones used by press photographers. Each time he took a picture, the flash popped and whined, the darkness was illuminated, and Phil Rafferty held up his hands in defence of his eyes.

How undignified, thought Prairie, *to lay on the side of a wet, dark road, to have your picture captured for eternity.* She took small comfort in the fact it was Constable Timms taking those pictures, and not some stranger from Golga. When the policeman had taken a picture from every conceivable angle, Timms covered the battered body of Briar Lee and as carefully as they could, he and the butcher lifted her onto a board, and then slid the board into the back of the refrigerated meat truck. A tear welled as Prairie thought of the young girl being driven back to her town, like a slab of butchered meat. As well-meaning and necessary as the situation was, it would be an awful thing to explain to Briar's parents.

They drove in a solemn convoy, the lights of the patrol car silently flashing blue, to the police station in Wheatsheaf to await the arrival of someone authoritative from Golga. Stan Banbury was parked in the driveway waiting for them.

'I can't get through,' he said. 'Road's blocked at the foot of Brewer's Hill. At least five massive gums have come down. They took out the bridge over the creek.'

'Oh, for God's sake,' said Constable Timms, losing his composure for a moment. He put his fingers to his temples and looked helplessly at his companions.

'I need the truck for the dawn deliveries,' said Rafferty, unhelpfully. 'She can't stay in there all night.'

'Right. Well, I suppose it will have to be the barrel cellar of the hotel,' said Timms peevishly.

'What?' Stan's eyes bulged.

'That's right,' said Prairie helpfully, 'In the olden days, the cellar of the local hotel actually used to double as the town morgue, because it was cold and stopped the deceased from rotting.'

'Next you'll be telling me that autopsies were carried out on the bar!' said Stan incredulously.

Prairie nodded. 'Yes,' she said. 'That's right. Oh, Stan, I know this is awful, but it's an awful situation. Briar was a member of this town, and someone's done a terrible, terrible thing. We need to look after her now. None of us could protect her when… well, you know. But we can be a little compassionate and protect her now, can't we?'

Stan blushed at Prairie's round, earnest eyes pleading for his help. He shuffled from foot to foot. 'Yeah, I guess so. But Dad's not going to like it much. You saw how he reacted to Heck Johnson's sheep on the bar floor.'

'In times like this,' said Emmanuel Timms, drawing himself up to full height, 'the constabulary must take charge and make orders as necessary to…get done…whatever is needed…to be done. I'll speak to Arthur about it. I'm sure he'll be reasonable.'

13

The Silo

'You've got to be bloody joking!' Arthur Banbury roared at Emmanuel Timms.

'Please Arthur, be reasonable. It's only until we can get the coroner here.'

'This is the local hotel, Timms, not a bloody mortuary!'

'I know that Arthur, but we have to keep the body somewhere cool to slow decomposition.'

'Decomposition? I'm not having a bloody decomposing body in my barrel cellar and that's final!'

'I'm afraid you have no choice,' said Timms. 'Arthur Banbury, I'm placing you under arrest for failing to assist Police in the matter of the investigation into the homicide of Briar Lee.' Timms made a show of reaching for his handcuffs.

Arthur Banbury looked as though he'd been slapped. His eyes bulged in his ruddy face. 'You can't be serious? Put those fucking things away.'

'Oh Arthur!' wailed Felice. 'For pity's sake!'

'A woman has died,' said Timms hotly. 'A member of this town. In the worst possible way. Murdered. And left in the middle of the highway to be obliterated like roadkill!' His eyes blazed like embers. Prairie saw that the evening was taking a terrible toll on him. She herself wanted nothing more than to crawl into bed and pull the covers up over her head and to pretend this had all been just a horrible dream.

'Please Arthur,' she said, gently. 'It's all gone so terribly wrong tonight. For Briar's killer to be caught, her body must be preserved until it can be examined by the coroner.'

'Why can't she stay in the meat truck?'

'I need the truck for deliveries at five A.M.!' Phil Rafferty protested. 'I can't very well turn up to the Hiskins Farm or the Johnsons with a dead body in the back, can I? Wouldn't be very hygienic, would it?'

'I don't see how it's any different from all the other dead carcasses you have in there,' Arthur retorted.

'Oh, here you go, Mrs Hiskins,' said Rafferty, miming a delivery. 'Here's your side of beef. That? Oh, don't worry about that. That's just Briar Lee – we scraped her off the highway last night.'

'*Oh, for the love of God!*' thundered Felice. 'Will you stop talking about her like she's a slab of meat! That's Briar Lee! A young girl who, for all her faults, I am sure did *not* deserve to die the way she did. Now, you men just think about her poor old mum and how her heart's going to break when she finds out that, not only has her baby girl died at the hands of some demented madman, but we squabbled about whether she should wait for the coroner in the butcher's truck or on the pub floor! Shame on you both.' Felice's eyes filled with tears.

'I can't bear it,' she said, wiping her nose on her sleeve. 'It's just too much.' She sniffed, squared her shoulders and tossed back her wavy chestnut mane. '*I* am the landlady of this establishment, and *I'll* say what's what. Stanley, help Phil bring Briar down into the cellar. Be careful of those steps. Arthur will move some barrels and clear a space. And be gentle with her. She was somebody's daughter.'

O   O   O

It was past ten o'clock when Prairie finally got into bed, but she slept fitfully. Every time she was on the threshold of sleep, her thoughts drifted back to the body of Briar Lee in the cellar below. She wondered how Gil was. She hadn't seen him since he'd left dinner, but she supposed he'd heard the news. It would be all around town by now. At least it wouldn't have travelled further, Prairie observed, with the telegraph lines down on Brewer's Hill.

She rose at dawn, dressed warmly and took her sketchpad downstairs. The bar was dark and quiet. Felice was usually in the kitchen humming away by now. Prairie guessed she and Arthur must have slept late. As she passed the bar on her way to the door, she glanced down at the trap door which led to the cellar. She shuddered and hurried out to Baby Blue. She had promised to meet Constable Timms at the silo to help him conduct as thorough examination of the area as the weather – and their limited resources – would permit.

She arrived just as the sun was colouring the sky – another vivid red, heralding more angry weather. She parked Baby Blue on the side of the road and while she waited, took up her pad and began to sketch the outlines of the silo in dark graphite. Although unhappy circumstances brought her here, she marvelled at the structure. It was an impressive collection of buildings. How wonderful, she thought, if they could be painted. A towering mural in mauves and pinks of Blush Lake at sunset, perhaps? Every now and then her eyes darted back to the side of the road where Briar Lee's lifeless body had lain just hours ago. She forced them back to her work.

The rapidly rising sun had washed out the red and was streaking the sky fairy-floss pink when Timms' patrol car crested the rise ahead. He looked as though he hadn't slept for a week.

'I'm not sure this is proper,' he said. 'I'm not sure I'm following protocol by allowing a civilian to assist in a murder inquiry.'

'I'm only helping you to look for clues or evidence around the silo,' Prairie reasoned. 'You can't be expected to do it all alone, and who else is there to help? I won't touch anything. If I see anything suspicious, I'll call you right over.'

Timms thought about it and relented. He wasn't going to admit it, but the weight of the past two days was crushing him. He felt very, *very* alone and was glad of Prairie's company.

'Alright then, Miss Marple,' he said.

Prairie bowed. 'I have always preferred Hercule Poirot,' she said solemnly. 'Come along, Captain Hastings.'

It was decided that Timms would start at the point in the road where Sam Swallow had hit the brakes of his truck. Prairie would make an initial circuit of the silos.

'What exactly am I looking for?' she asked. Timms shrugged uncertainly. Blood, perhaps? A slit throat would produce a lot of blood. Although, he said, it was quite possible that the murder had taken place far away from Wheatsheaf, and the body of Briar Lee merely dumped at the silos. They were, after all, the gateway to the town where she belonged. As such, he said, they might not find anything at all.

As she picked her way around the buildings of Golden Grain's Wheatsheaf store, she looked for anything that might have been out of the ordinary. But she quickly conceded that as she didn't know what 'ordinary' was supposed to look like at a grain silo, this was going to be difficult. The silo saw activity mainly during the harvest season, when trucks like Sam Swallow's came and went at all hours of the day until last light. It was possible that nobody had been at the silo since Summer.

Prairie stalked past the testing stand and the weighbridge, being careful not to catch her shoes in the grate. She was glad she was wearing her tennis shoes. During harvest, trucks laden with grain pulled up to the weighbridge and deposited their golden treasure down into the bowels of the silo through these grates. Giant augers transported the grain upwards, and the grain elevators moved the grain from the silos into empty train carriages waiting patiently in the railway sidings.

The long grain shed looked as though it had not been disturbed since the harvest ended. The door was padlocked. Prairie looked carefully in the mud for footprints, tyre tracks, signs of a struggle, but saw nothing other than her own footprints from the night before.

She turned her attention to the out-buildings and noticed the troublesome door, which she had shut last night. It stood ajar.

Carefully, she pulled the door open. Mercifully, nothing jumped out this time. The jerrycans lay there in a jumble, with some old paint tins and rags. She turned at footsteps crunching across the gravel towards her.

'Anything?' Timms was hopeful. Prairie shook her head.

'Nothing so far. But perhaps you'd best take a second look. I may have missed something.' They made a circuit of the site together.

'There was nothing on the road, except the skid marks from Sam's truck. The blasted rain has probably washed away any evidence. Tell me, Prairie, what were Miss Lee's last movements as you recall them?'

'Well,' said Prairie, thinking carefully. 'I met her in the bar at the Harvest Hotel on Tuesday. She had the day off and she and Olive were there when I arrived. That would have been about five o'clock I guess.'

'You went there after work?'

'Yes – but not straight after my shift at the exchange,' said Prairie, thinking. 'I had to work back a bit longer because Mr Peterson fired Mabel Wattage, so I had to cover for longer than usual. But afterwards, I went to the *Granary Caff*. Mabel was there, and she was terribly upset. I sat with her for a couple of hours, I think.'

'How did Miss Lee seem to you?'

'Oh, perfectly fine. Briar-esque, I'd say.'

'What do you mean by that?'

'Just…herself. Full of fun and mischief. She was pleased with herself. She'd had the day off and spent it shopping.'

'In Wheatsheaf?'

Prairie nodded. 'I presume so.' She thought. 'She'd gone to the mechanic. She'd had some car trouble –'

'Car trouble?'

'Yes – Olive knows more about that than I do. Oh – and the jewellery store. Evans & Son. She'd bought a beautiful diamond bracelet.'

'What time did she leave the bar?'

Prairie thought again. 'You know, I have absolutely no idea. Olive left us to go to her shift.'

'What time was that?'

'Well, she was on the six o'clock, so maybe twenty minutes to six? Gil Sanders joined us then. He's a geologist at the salt works out on the lake.' Prairie blushed despite herself. 'The three of us sat and chatted, but it was all cut short by Heck Johnson bringing in his dead sheep.'

'Ah, yes!' said Timms, nodding. 'Very unsavoury business that. I wonder if the vet's been to look at the carcass yet.'

'Well, I hope to goodness the vet finds the sheep died of natural causes because the town is being very unpleasant to Gil. The other salt workers have had to leave! Gil's car has been vandalised – he's very upset.'

'That was about six o'clock that Heck Johnson showed up, wasn't it? I escorted him out at about twenty-past.'

'I don't actually remember seeing Briar after the affray. Gil left the bar as soon as you took Mr Johnson away, and I followed him up to the balcony. He was very upset, as I said. I was trying to calm him down. Now that I think about it, I don't think I even said good-bye to Briar. I feel awful about that now,' said Prairie.

'There was a lot going on – and you weren't to know it would all end up like this,' said Timms gently.

They were now standing directly in front of the door to the little outbuilding. Timms looked at the ground. 'Ooh look here! This area has seen some recent activity. There's a bally lot of footprints!' He squatted down, examining them.

'Oh,' said Prairie. 'I'm afraid that was probably me. I waited for you by that triangular building last night, and I marched around on the spot to keep warm. But this door started banging in the wind, so I came over to investigate. I shut the door firmly last night, I know I did – but it was open again this morning.'

Timms opened the door. The rising sun cast a beautiful beam of orange warmth into the interior, lighting the gloom and dust. And it came to rest glinting on an object that may otherwise have remained hidden from view.

'What's that?' said Prairie, pointing to the dirt by the threshold. Timms stooped to examine something imbedded there. He took a pen out of his breast pocket and picked the object up. A small key on a plain ring dangled on the tip of the pen.

'What have we here?' Timms wondered aloud. 'Did you drop a key last night?'

'I don't think so.' Prairie checked her purse. The keys to her hotel room and Baby Blue were all present and accounted for. Timms squinted at it. It was an odd shape, and he felt he'd seen it somewhere before. It bore no significant markings though. He pulled a small plastic bag from his trouser pocket and dropped the key in.

'Hopefully, Barry Skipton will be able to tell me what kind of lock this key fits. Best not to say anything to anybody about our little search, Miss Humble. It is, after all, a murder investigation.'

14

Skeleton Key

Felice and Arthur were in the bar, talking in hushed tones. 'How long is it going to be down there?' Arthur grumbled.

'Shh, Arthur. *She.*'

'I need a bloody crate of tonic brought up. I'm not going down there while *she's* there.' They both jumped as Prairie pushed open the door to the bar.

'Love a duck!' Felice whinnied. 'You damn near gave me a heart-attack, Prairie love.'

'I'm sorry, Felice.'

'Don't mind us. We're just at sevens and eights what with –' Felice cocked her head towards the trap door. 'You know.'

Prairie nodded. 'Has Gil been down yet?'

'Oh, my darling,' Felice's face was suddenly stricken. 'I'm afraid you've missed him. He's gone.'

'Gone? Gone where?'

'Came down first thing this morning, bags all packed. Said he wanted to settle up. I'm sorry, love. I thought you would have known?'

'But, why? Where did he go?'

'I think it's getting a bit much. You know, the business with Heck Johnson. And when I told him about Briar Lee, well, he couldn't settle the cheque fast enough.'

'Has he gone back to Golga?' Prairie thought she might burst into tears, and this surprised her.

'I don't know, my love.' Felice patted Prairie's hand. Prairie stared down at the perfectly manicured, too-long red tips of Felice Banbury's fingers.

○ ○ ○

With a paper cup of hot coffee in one hand and a piece of buttered toast between her teeth, Prairie yanked open the driver's side door of Baby Blue – a little too forcefully – and slid in behind the wheel. She didn't blame Gil – but she allowed herself a pang of annoyance that he hadn't stayed long enough to tell her himself. Truly dreadful hours had recently passed. There was so much she wanted to talk over with him. Her shift didn't start for a couple of hours, so she pointed Baby Blue north and drove towards Blush Lake. She didn't really know what else to do.

A figure in a yellow raincoat was walking along the shoulder of the road, where the road left town just past Reynold's garage. Prairie recognised the lumbering gait. She slowed the car and wound down the window.

'Hello Agnes,' she called. 'Would you like a ride?' Agnes looked startled but her face spread into a grin at the sight of Prairie.

'Oh hello, Prairie,' she said. 'I don't want to trouble you.'

'No trouble,' said Prairie. 'Hop in!' Much to her surprise and delight, Agnes considered the proposition and then walked around the bonnet to the passenger door.

'Thank you,' she said. 'I've just been to the church to talk to Father Childers about the funeral. I thought I might take a walk out to Blush Lake to clear my head. I've been thinking a lot about it since your visit.'

'Wonderful,' said Prairie. 'I was actually on the way there myself.'

They drove past the Comfrey home and past the exchange, past barren fields until Baby Blue pulled into the gravel parking lot. The pink lake spread out before them. She was much deeper after the night's deluge and resplendent in the golden light of the still morning. Agnes stared through the windscreen, transfixed.

'Shall we walk down to the shore?'

Agnes nodded, dumbly. The air was cool, but at least it was still. They left Baby Blue and trudged through the samphire and saltbush. The sand was boggy underfoot. Prairie led Agnes to the crystallised outcrop.

'I like to sit here and sketch,' she said. They sat down together and stared over the vast expanse of pink, salty water. A bank of clouds gathered in the distance and were reflected as great white drifts on the surface. With no wind to disturb the peace, the lake was a smooth, perfect mirror.

'I can't remember the last time I was here,' Agnes said. 'It must be years.' She inhaled deeply. The briny tang of the inland sea was a heady mixture. 'Mother hated this place. Said it reeked of dead fish and sorrow. I'm not sure what she meant by that. I suppose I could always have come here by myself, but there never seemed to be time.'

Prairie cocked her head quizzically and Agnes went on. 'Mother required rather a degree of attention,' she continued, answering the unasked question. 'There was always something to do, from sun-up to bedtime.' She stared out at the horizon and said quietly. 'I'm afraid life has been a bit of a blur.'

'We get so busy sometimes,' said Prairie, 'that we literally do forget to stop and smell the roses. I know it's a bit twee, but there is something to be said for pausing. I do it such a lot,' she went on. 'Perhaps that's why I like to sketch. I'm forever looking at clouds and sunsets. Or the way light plays on a certain object at different times of the day. I'm overcome sometimes by a need to capture it. To put it on paper in case I ever forget.'

'What a wonderful sentiment,' said Agnes.

'How are you getting along?' Prairie asked gently.

'Oh. Along. Father Childers has been very kind. And very patient. I've been trying to make some arrangements for the service. It's hard to set a date without Mother's body. I wonder when she'll come home. It would have been much simpler had Mother told me some of the things she'd like to have had though.'

'She never discussed her final wishes?'

'Oh yes – she told me to build a pyre at the bottom of the garden and set her alight, but I rather think there'd be a law against that.'

Prairie laughed and clapped a hand over her mouth. Agnes smiled. 'Mother despises – despised – the Church. She said they were all thieves and molesters. Father O'Dougherty behaved so appallingly when he was here, that he gave her more than enough ammunition. Father Childers was always very patient with us despite her views. I doubt many will come to the service,' she said, sadly.

'I'll be there,' said Prairie, gently. 'And so will Constable Timms. You, you are religious, Agnes?'

'I take comfort in God,' said Agnes softly. 'I rather wanted to be a nun when I was younger. I think I would have been quite good at it. My father was a religious man, Catholic. Mother behaved herself back then.'

'What did your father do?' asked Prairie.

'He was a granary worker,' said Agnes. 'He worked for Golden Grain, like so many of the people around here. I used to love going to work with him. He'd let me ride in the truck and play about in the silos. I loved watching the trucks tipping their grain. I always wanted to swim in it! Imagine that.'

'I should think that would be rather dangerous,' Prairie observed.

'Oh yes, very dangerous,' said Agnes, quietly. 'My father always kept a very close eye on me. Silos are dangerous things. He died when I was nine. I hate them now. Can't bear to look at them.'

'I'm so sorry,' said Prairie quietly and shuddered. 'I've had rather enough of silos myself.'

Agnes looked at her quizzically. Prairie felt compelled to explain. 'I've been helping Constable Timms.' Agnes stared at her blankly. 'Briar Lee. You know she was found at the silo last night?'

Agnes shook her head. 'No. Found doing what?'

'Oh,' Prairie suddenly felt awkward and remembered Constable Timms warning. 'She, Briar, was found on the road by the silos last night. She's…she died.'

'Oh dear!' gasped Agnes. 'Oh, how awful! What happened?'

Prairie was careful. 'I'm not sure,' she said. 'The lines are down at Brewer's Hill, so we have to wait for the coroner.'

'Yes,' said Agnes. 'I noticed my telephone wasn't working again when I tried to call Father Childers this morning. How truly awful. That ill wind certainly blew no good. Mother always said, 'Beware the North wind, for it drives the Devil before it.''

Prairie smiled softly, thinking of Felice. 'Was your mother superstitious Agnes?'

Agnes chuckled. 'A little, I guess. I know the townsfolk thought she was a witch. She was certainly spiritual, but not religious. People can be so cruel.' Agnes seemed lost in her memories of another time. She turned to Prairie suddenly.

'I'm so sorry Mother was rude when you brought the cake to the house. It was so kind of you. I'm afraid kindness is something we rarely experience. I expect Mother was not sure how to act.' She sighed and turned her gaze back out to the vast expanse before her. 'They hate us, you know. The people in the town. Well, they hated my mother. They tolerate me, sometimes. Father Childers is the only person in Wheatsheaf who was always pleasant to Mother. Not that it ever got him any gratitude.' She smiled ruefully. 'I consider myself fortunate to have his support at this time.'

'Not much point in being a priest if you can't love all your flock, even when they are being unlovable,' Prairie observed. 'Turning the other cheek and all that. Would you like me to take you home? I must be getting on to the salt works.' She stood up and brushed the salt off her dress. Agnes didn't move.

'No – thank you,' she said, taking a deep breath and closing her eyes. 'I think I'll take the air a little longer. The lake and I have some reacquainting to do.' She opened her eyes and smiled at Prairie. 'Thank you, Miss Humble. You are kind, indeed.'

○ ○ ○

Emmanuel Timms was a man not prone to gambling. Under the present circumstances, however, he allowed himself a wager and decided that he was damned if he did, and damned if he did not. Either way, the coroner would be sure to have stern words when he was finally able to summon him. So, he thought, better to have some record of evidence before decomposition set in, than none to offer the coroner whatsoever.

It was cold in the cellar of the Harvest Hotel, and it reeked of beer and damp earth. Another smell was discernible, faint and coppery, and he tried to close his nostrils against it as far as possible. The body of Briar Lee lay on a trestle table covered in a white sheet. Timms sighed and with gloved hands, pulled a surgical mask up over his nose and slipped the sheet back.

Her face, once beautiful and clear, was now mottled and blue. Her lustrous blonde hair was dark. Strands stuck out from her head like bits of seaweed. Timms walked around the table with his camera. The flash popped and popped again. He focused the lens upon her face. And now her neck, capturing the ragged cut, which ran from just under her left ear to the windpipe. He shuddered and wished that Miss Humble were here. He would have appreciated her level head and light humour in this moment, but he knew he could never expose a civilian to such a grisly task – least of all sweet, kind Prairie – so it must be his alone to bear. He swallowed and leaned forward, sticking the lens of the camera close to the cut, and focused. *Pop! Flash! Whrrrr!*

The windpipe did not appear to be severed. But he guessed the carotid artery certainly would have been. He jotted down some notes on his pad, detailing the pictures he had taken. *Ragged cut left ear to windpipe. Assailant right-handed? Jagged instrument – serrated knife? Cause of death – blood-loss occasioned by severed carotid artery?*

'I apologise for this, Miss Lee,' he whispered to the corpse, 'but I think this is necessary, under the circumstances.' He took a pair of scissors and carefully cut open her blouse and the front of her black skirt. He blushed at the site of her pale torso, her lacey white brassiere and matching knickers, now filthy. He tried not to focus on the dead woman's breasts and instead busied himself examining her torso for bruises or other marks. The impact of Sam Swallow's truck was obvious. Timms guessed the ribs were fractured, as obviously was the right leg. Without conducting a postmortem, he couldn't be sure, and as he was not about to do that here (he did not have the right instruments for one thing, nor would he have known what to do with them for another), he busied himself with sketching and taking more pictures.

He had a magnifying glass and holding it at arm's length, he combed her body from head to toe, looking for fibres or anything out of the ordinary. In Briar Lee's hair, close to her scalp, he found traces of what looked like sawdust. Using long tweezers, he plucked the remnants from her head and dropped them into a small plastic bag. Thinking hard about what else the detectives in his favoured novels looked for, he gently picked up her hands and examined them one by one. He was looking for anything under her fingernails. They were dirty and some of the pink nails were ragged. The fingernail of her right ring-finger had been torn clean off. Blood caked the nailbed. Miss Lee had been particular about her manicures. Had she fought for her life with these hands? A heaviness in his chest threatened to rise, like a buoyant object in water, not properly weighed down. Had he let it break the surface, it could have been a sob, but he plunged it back down to the depths where a hundred dead emotions dwelled. He had nothing to swab her hands with and cursed quietly. He decided to take some photographs instead.

He looked at the sole of her single, right shoe. Stan Banbury had picked it up from the side of the road. It was a flat-soled slipper, pale pink, made of leather. It resembled a ballet shoe. Possibly, she had been wearing it at the time she was struck by Sam Swallow's truck; certainly at the time of the murder. There was no sign of the other shoe, which led Timms to believe that she had been murdered at another site and the body brought to the middle of the road at the silos and dumped. He scribbled this down in his notepad. The sole of the shoe was caked in mud. He took a photograph of the slipper and placed it into another plastic bag. Eventually, not really knowing what else to do, he covered Briar Lee's body with the sheet once more. He peeled off his gloves, took off his mask and placed them both into another bag for disposal, collected his camera and exhibits, and mounted the cellar stairs, leaving Briar Lee to her dark repose.

○　○　○

Barry Skipton turned the small silver key over in his big, calloused hands. Timms had taken the precaution of dropping it into a clear plastic bag in case there were any fingerprints on it. The farrier nodded thoughtfully.

'Not one of mine, I don't think, but I know what it is.' He and Timms stood in the small forge at his farm on the outskirts of Wheatsheaf. Here, the local farrier fashioned horseshoes and mended the town's tools. But he also cut their keys and picked their locks when required. Timms was glad to be out of the Banbury's cellar. He had driven out to the farm with the window down the whole way, despite the chilly air. The slight scent of decay would just not leave him. Here in the forge, it was warm and smelled of hot iron and hay. Quite the contrast to the cellar, he observed.

'What is it?' he asked.

'Skeleton key,' said Skipton. 'See here?' He pointed to the lower end of the shaft of the key. 'A regular key would have teeth along here, but see how this one just has this bit here at the bottom? That's how you tell it's a skeleton key. Opens multiple types of locks. This here,' he said, pointing again to the bottom of the key, 'is the essential part. Helps it to bypass the wards in a lock.'

'Wards?'

'The devices that tumble in a lock, so as you can't open it without the right key.'

'This is like a master key?' asked Timms.

Skipton nodded. 'Yup.'

'A master key for what though?' Timms pressed. Skipton rubbed his chin thoughtfully.

'Well, it ain't real big, so I'd say a smaller lock.'

'Like a padlock?'

'Hmm. Maybe a bigger padlock. A chest, perhaps? Doesn't look like it'd be a house key. I'd expect that to be bigger.'

'Any idea which locksmith might have cut this key?'

Skipton turned it over and held it up to the light. The key was devoid of any kind of marking. He shook his head. 'Could have been cut by anyone, at any time. It doesn't look new. I just know it's not one of mine.'

'Thanks, Barry,' said Timms, repocketing the key and turned to take his leave.

'Damn shame about that Lee girl,' said Skipton.

'Yes. Yes, it is.'

'Hope you catch him,' said Skipton, narrowing his slate-grey eyes.

'Yes,' said Timms again. 'It's a damned nuisance with these lines being down.'

As he got into his patrol car and pulled away from the forge, he wondered how many keys in Wheatsheaf and the surrounding countryside were not cut by Barry Skipton. 'Probably hundreds,' he said to himself and sighed.

O   O   O

Prairie left Agnes Comfrey to her reveries on the shore of Blush Lake. She and Baby Blue headed further north on the highway for another three miles until she came to Saltworks Road. She slowed at the gatehouse and spoke to the guard.

'I'm looking for Gil Sanders,' she explained. 'Is it possible to see him?' The guard motioned her into the little parking lot and summoned Gil on a radio. Prairie waited for what seemed an age before Gil's tall frame strode out of the administrative building towards her car. He leaned in through the open window. He looked tired and gaunt.

'You're lucky to have caught me,' he said. 'I've been out on the pan all morning. I've just come in for lunch.'

'I'm afraid I didn't think to bring something to eat,' said Prairie, apologetically. At the thought of food, her stomach pulled like a tide going out to sea. Gil smiled and held up a paper bag.

'I'll split my sandwich with you, if you like?'

'Hop in.' Prairie leaned over and pushed open the passenger door, and the geologist slid in beside her. 'I've been worried about you,' she said. 'Felice told me you'd left the hotel.'

Gil fished out half of a ham and pickle sandwich and handed it to her, taking a bite of the other half. He nodded as he chewed, swallowed and then said, 'I'm sorry, Prairie. I had every intention of phoning you tonight at the hotel. I just can't stay in town right now. The company agrees it's not safe. They don't want any trouble and neither do I. It's only a matter of time before someone takes a swing at me.'

'You couldn't have phoned,' said Prairie ruefully. 'The telegraph lines are down at Brewer's Hill. Lord knows when they'll be fixed. We can't get to Golga by road either. Stan Banbury couldn't get across the creek.'

'What was he doing on the road to Golga? Say, has the vet come to look at Heck Johnson's sheep yet?'

'Oh Gil, you don't know, do you?'

'Know what?'

Prairie took a deep breath. She was so tired she felt as though she could shatter. 'We found Briar Lee last night, Gil. Well, that's to say Sam Swallow found her. On the road, near the silo.'

Prairie watched the colour drain from Gil's face. He stopped chewing and swallowed hard. 'What do you mean *found her*?'

'Remember I told you that she hadn't turned up for her shift yesterday morning? I didn't think you were paying attention – you seemed so distracted – and I don't blame you, what with your car being vandalised like that, but anyway, she didn't turn up for her shift and I couldn't get into the exchange because the Night Boy got annoyed when Briar didn't show at six o'clock and left.' Gil stared, open-mouthed as Prairie rushed on. 'Oh, Gil. It's been such an awful night. After you went upstairs, Sam Swallow came into the hotel claiming that he'd run over a girl. Constable Timms, Stan Banbury, Olive and I went out there in the rain –'

'Out where?'

'To the *silo*. And she was there, Gil. By the side of the road. Oh Gil, it was horrible.' Prairie covered her eyes at the memory.

'What happened?' Gil's voice was barely audible. Prairie took a deep breath.

'Someone killed her, Gil. Someone slit her throat.'

'Oh my God!' Gil was stunned. 'She was…why would anyone do that?' He turned to Prairie. 'That must have been such an awful thing for you to see.'

Prairie nodded. 'It was horrible, and I really shouldn't be talking about it. But it was *me* who noticed her throat had been cut. Awful, ragged wound, it was. Sam Swallow thought he'd killed her when he ran her over, but Constable Timms thinks it was likely that she was already dead. Someone killed her, Gil. Someone murdered her and left her there in the road like *roadkill.*'

Gil sat back in stunned silence.

'I've been wanting to speak to you so badly even though Constable Timms has warned me not to say anything,' Prairie went on. 'When I came back to the hotel this morning, Felice said you'd gone.'

'I knocked at your door early this morning,' said Gil, quietly. 'When you didn't answer, I looked for Baby Blue, but she was gone.'

'Yes,' said Prairie vaguely. 'I went out to draw the silo at sunrise.' Her sketchpad was on the back seat. She leaned across and showed Gil. He smiled.

'These are so good, Prairie.' He was silent for a moment. 'Prairie…'

'Yes.'

Gil shook his head. 'It's nothing.'

'Are you really going to stay here at the saltworks, Gil? How long for?'

Gil shrugged. 'For the rest of my assignment, I guess. Unless the vet tells Heck Johnson and the rest of the town that I didn't poison his sheep. I've still got a few weeks to go yet.'

'Where will you sleep?'

'There's a little room off my lab. It's not big, but I made a cot up in there. If it gets too cramped, I can always use one of the huts out the back. Workers sometimes stay out there. I have a key to one of them.' Gil pulled out a set of keys and began to flick through them. 'I thought it was on here,' he said to himself. 'Oh no, that's right. It's on another ring.' He felt in his each of his trouser pockets, and finding them empty, patted his breast pocket.

'That's strange,' he said. 'Surely I haven't lost it somewhere.'

The colour drained from Prairie's face. She turned as white as the salt pan before her.

15

Ozone and Petrichor

Olive Wellshorn's car was parked at the exchange when Prairie arrived for her midday shift.

'I didn't know whether to turn up or not,' she said, peeling off her coat and headscarf. It was deliciously warm inside. 'Are the lines up yet?'

Olive shook her head. 'No, but they are working on them. A party from the town has been clearing those trees off the road at Brewer's Hill. I dare say we'll see Mr Peterson at first light. He'll probably swim across the creek.' She rolled her eyes. Prairie noticed dark half-circles underneath them. She sank into a chair.

'You look how I feel,' she said, exhausted.

'Cuppa?'

'Please. I could murder….' Prairie groaned inwardly and let the word hang awkwardly. Olive gave a wry smile.

'Strange times,' she said, 'call for large measures.' She held up a small bottle of whiskey. 'I think we could both do with this.' Prairie smiled gratefully.

What did your key look like, Gil? she had asked uneasily, dreading the answer, holding her breath. *It was small,* he'd said. *It was silver.* Prairie's heart sank. *Where do you think you could have lost it?* she asked, feeling oddly detached from her body. He'd shrugged. *Hopefully not out on the salt pan or I'll never find it,* he'd answered. Her urge to get away was almost maniacal. She was grateful for her upcoming shift. She'd lied and said that it started at eleven and must get going. *Will you come back soon?* he'd asked. *Yes, oh yes,* she'd promised.

'Penny for them,' said Olive, placing a steaming mug of coffee in front of her. The alcoholic vapours pierced Prairie's sinuses and made her eyes water, but she sipped the scalding brew anyway and shook her head in defeat. Olive nodded and looked out the window. 'It's all so surreal,' she said. 'There is almost no point in us being here, but I don't know what else to do. I couldn't just sit at home waiting. Waiting for news. Waiting for the lines to be up. I can't stand my own company at the moment.'

Prairie nodded. 'I know that feeling. Say Olive, did Briar have a boyfriend?' she asked, to keep her mind off Gil. 'She was so young and pretty, surely there must have been someone special?'

Olive shrugged. 'I dare say she had one or two. Or many. I know she had dates with some of the young men around town. She was with the mechanic's apprentice for a bit – Eli – but I don't think it was ever anything serious. Briar was…flighty.'

Prairie cocked her head quizzically.

'She liked to flirt,' said Olive, 'but not necessarily commit. She was forever telling me stories.'

'She always had such fine clothes and accessories,' Prairie mused, remembering the bracelet and midnight blue stilettos. 'How did she ever afford such things? I've seen those shoes in the city, and they are not cheap.'

'I often wondered that myself,' said Olive. 'Her parents might give – have *given* her a generous allowance. I couldn't afford all that stuff on what the PMG pays me.'

'No,' said Prairie, an uneasy feeling growing in the back of her mind. 'Olive…' *No, I can't say it.*

'Mmhmm?' Olive sipped at her coffee.

'Is there anything I can do here? I'd like to see how Constable Timms is getting along.'

Olive shook her dark bob. 'I'm waiting on the technicians to dial in and tell me everything's good to go. I could die of old age waiting, of course…ohhh. I have to stop making these jokes.'

Prairie smiled sympathetically. 'I'll call back in a little while then – I'll bring you a sandwich.' She got up to retrieve her scarf and coat and turned back again.

'Olive…'

Olive looked up expectantly. Prairie thought back to that first night shift together, the first – and only – alongside Briar Lee. She recalled the wave of mistrust, now followed by a pang of guilt.

Once it's out there, it's out there, Prairie-girl. There's no putting it back in.

It was not uncommon, she reasoned, for telephonists to overhear conversations. As a senior telephonist, she often listened in to calls to check the quality of the line, or to assess the skills of the junior telephonists. Occasionally, while connecting a call to a party line, which was common, snippets of conversations came through the headset loud and clear. What was the difference?

The difference is that I never set out to eavesdrop.

'Did Briar ever work as an overseer?'

Olive shook her head and laughed. 'Can you imagine? Peterson would never have allowed that! She's lucky to have had the job at all.'

'So, never any reason for Briar to have listened in on calls?'

Olive shrugged. 'Not officially. But I guess we all do it occasionally.'

'I guess,' said Prairie. 'Ham and cheese alright?'

O   O   O

The patrol car was backed into the driveway, ready to go at a moment's notice. Emmanuel Timms was at his desk, compiling a list of names. The plastic bags sat on the desk beside him. The bell over the door chimed. He got up and went to the front desk.

'Prairie! Are you alright?'

'Oh yes, yes, I'm fine. I just thought I'd see how you were getting on. There's nothing for me to do at the exchange right now. The lines are still down…'

'Damned nuisance,' Timms muttered irritably. 'Will they be down much longer?' Every hour that Briar Lee's body lay in the beer cellar increased his agitation ten-fold.

'The technicians are working on it now,' said Prairie. 'Although I don't know how long it will take to mend the bridge at Brewer's Hill. The equipment must be going across the river in a boat.'

Timms tapped a pencil on the desk and mulled it over in his mind.

'I wondered if there was anything I could do to help?'

Timms beckoned Prairie into his little office. A cactus and a wilting Peace Lily sat on his desk, along with a framed picture of a matronly woman. Prairie sat on a chair opposite. 'I'm compiling a list,' he said. 'I really should interview everyone in the town about their whereabouts on the night we discovered Miss Lee.'

'Do you have any idea about the time of death?'

Timms shook his head. 'Not really. Rather nasty wound she has. Severed the carotid artery on the left side – I *think*. I'm guessing she would have bled out rather quickly. So, I need to know where people were, and what they were up to – say, between six-thirty on Tuesday night, when you last recall seeing Miss Lee in the Harvest Hotel, and six o'clock Wednesday night when Sam Swallow *found* Miss Lee. Ooh!' he said. 'I suppose I'd better put Sam at the top of the list, not that I think he had anything to do with it, of course, but I probably shouldn't be saying that out loud, because this is a murder investigation – and of course, I'll need a formal statement from you, Miss Humble. I know we talked at the silo but, you know…'

'Of course.'

'Let me see. Who else?' he chewed on the end of his pencil.

'Well Olive Wellshorn was there with us before Heck Johnson came in. She can at least corroborate some of my version of events. And she probably knows Briar better than most. And possibly Mr

Peterson, as her employer, of course.' *He hated Briar Lee,* thought Prairie. *But did he hate her enough to kill her?*

'Of course.' *Scribble, scribble.*

'The jeweller – Evans & Son – she went in there on her day off to buy the bracelet.'

'Ah yes, good, good.' *Scratch, scribble.*

'The mechanic – she picked up her car that day too,' said Prairie. 'And I overheard the most dreadful conversation between Jim Reynolds and his apprentice on Sunday morning. I wonder now if they were talking about Briar…'

There were two more names she thought she should list, but Prairie just couldn't bring herself to say *Mabel Wattage* and *Gil Sanders.* She glanced down at the plastic bags on the desk. She saw the shoe and the small silver key, and her stomach lurched.

As if reading her thoughts, Timms said 'Skeleton key.'

'Pardon?'

'It's a skeleton key – so Barry Skipton tells me. Used for opening a range of locks.'

'Like a master key?'

'Exactly like a master key. I'm confounded about the shoe,' he said nonplussed. 'Where's the other? We made a complete circuit of that place but found only one shoe. Where's her left shoe?'

Prairie looked at the ballet slipper in its plastic bag. 'Are you sure this is her shoe? I've never seen Briar in anything but heels.'

Timms shrugged. 'Stan Banbury found it by the side of the road, on the night Sam…I suppose if Miss Lee had been brought to the silos from elsewhere, perhaps it came off in the killer's vehicle. Or at the place he killed her,' Timms went on, proposing a theory to answer his own question. 'I'd like to get an analysis on this stuff I picked out of her hair.' He picked up the plastic bag. 'It looks like sawdust.'

'You didn't…?' Prairie was unable to say it.

'Autopsy? Goodness me, no, Miss Humble. I don't have the tools, for one thing. Or the training, for another.' *Or the stomach,* he thought.

'It does look like sawdust,' said Prairie. 'Or chaff?'

'Pardon?'

'Chaff. From the wheat. Given we found her at a grain silo, could it be wheat?'

Timms looked at the bag, looked at the telephonist, and sunk back in his chair, deflated.

○   ○   ○

Leaving the police station, Prairie stopped in at the grocers. Jonetta Williams, the grocer's wife, greeted Prairie through pinched lips. She looked like she was chewing a wasp. And when Prairie went next door to the *Granary Caff,* she quickly wished she hadn't.

'Probably killed that young lass too.'

'*Sshh!*' A table of three looked at her and bowed their heads towards their teacups. Prairie glared at them on her way to the counter.

'Pay them no mind, love,' whispered Rosie-Mandy. 'Not having the lines up is killing them.' She bit her lip. 'Sorry, I…'

'It doesn't matter,' said Prairie, irritably. 'Just a ham and cheese sandwich, please. Actually, could you make it three? With pickles. I'll wait outside.' She glared at the table on her way out and thought she heard a snigger before another '*Sshh!*'

Waiting for the sandwich, she crossed the street and browsed the glittering object in the window of *Evans & Son.* Her eye was drawn to a bracelet that looked very much like the one Briar had shown off that night at the hotel. Prairie pushed the door open, rousing Evans the Elder from a midday nap.

'How much is that bracelet in the window?' she asked. 'The one just at the front. Are those diamonds?'

The jeweller shuffled to the window and pulled out a blue velvet case. The delicate bracelet glinted brilliantly. 'Real diamonds,' he said, 'Set in real silver. It's a hundred and fifty dollars.'

'Oh my!' Prairie clutched her chest.

'Would you like to try it on?' Mesmerised, Prairie extended her arm, and Mr Evans clasped the bracelet around her slender wrist. She turned it this way and that, watching the way the string of diamonds caught and refracted the light. 'It's exquisite,' she said.

'Miss Lee seemed to think so,' said Evans quietly. Prairie swallowed. She held out her wrist and allowed the jeweller to take it off again.

'Thank you,' she said.

Hurriedly pushing the door open, she ran headlong into Simone MacMurrough. The girl held out a paper bag. 'Your sandwiches.'

Prairie took them, gratefully. 'Thank you, Simone,' she said and smiled.

Simone stared at her. 'People are mean sometimes,' she said solemnly, then turned and crossed the street. Prairie watched her disappear back into the café. She lowered her groceries carefully into the foot-well of Baby Blue and tossed the sandwiches onto the seat, slid behind the wheel and gunned the engine. Baby Blue headed south down Grain Street.

O   O   O

The silos, when they loomed into view, were a half-expected surprise. Indicating right, Prairie swung across the highway into the gravel service road and pulled Baby Blue to a halt. She sat there, blinking.

What am I doing here?

But even as she asked herself the question, she was out the door and heading across the damp gravel. Crossing the silo yard to the door to the utility room, Prairie was stabbed by a sudden pang of guilt. *This is an active crime scene*, she thought. *I have no business being here without Constable Timms.* She looked about, almost willing the patrol car to crest the rise, but the road was quiet. Prairie reasoned that her footprints were already all over the place, so a few more wouldn't hurt. She was just looking – she wouldn't touch anything. Looking for what though? Prairie knew very well what she was looking for and brushed the thought aside.

She scoured the area keeping an eye out for Briar's left slipper. Pulling her sleeve down over her right hand, Prairie carefully opened the door to the utility room. She glanced down at the threshold, where the small silver key had lain, glinting in the morning sun. She squatted down, her eyes roving back and forth. She looked at the door jamb. Were there any marks, any signs of a struggle? Prairie chocked the door open wide to let in the light – and to satisfy herself that it wouldn't slam shut, trapping her in the darkness. Stepping into the utility room, she glanced about. The utility room was small and square. The jerrycans and paint tins were still there. Moving towards the furthest corner, Prairie noticed a door. A sign warned of a confined space beyond. The door was locked with a bolt and a padlock. The chaff in Briar's hair just didn't make sense. Out here, there was nothing but gravel, and mud, and a concrete floor. *Unless.*

Prairie glanced over at the long, low grain shed. Closing the door behind her, she stalked across the yard. She carefully examined the padlock. It was similar to the padlock in the utility room. Should she suggest to Timms that they use bolt-cutters to remove it?

Prairie circled the grain shed, looking for an alternative way in – or at the very least, a window; some way to see what lay beyond the locked door. But it was fruitless. The nagging voice telling her she'd no business being there eventually spoke louder than her curiosity and she sighed. Briar's slipper was nowhere to be seen. Prairie reluctantly returned to Baby Blue and pulled out of the service road. She drove north along the highway, back into Wheatsheaf and out to the exchange, as she'd meant to do in the beginning.

O   O   O

Olive was grateful for the sandwich and confirmed that the technicians were still hard at work. Prairie was dismissed until further notice. 'I'll resort to tried and tested means and send a carrier pigeon when your assistance is required,' Olive quipped.

Grim-faced, Prairie continued on her way out to the salt works. She told the guard at the gate she was there to deliver some groceries to Gil Sanders. The guard lifted the boom gate for her and pointed her in the direction of the office block. 'Mr Sanders will meet you in the foyer,' he told her. Prairie thanked him, took the bag of groceries and the sandwiches and stalked across the carpark.

It was warm in the foyer, a nice contrast to the chill of the air outside. Prairie's heart pounded as she stood on the pale green linoleum floor waiting for Gil. The foyer walls were white, white like salt and adorned with framed pictures of Blush Lake; at sunrise, at sunset, during a storm, after a storm. Always glistening, like a pink quartz jewel.

'Prairie!' Gil came towards her. 'I take it the lines are still down then?' He was wearing a lab coat. Even in a lab coat, he looked handsome. Prairie smiled stiffly and held out the bag of groceries.

'I brought you these,' she said. 'I thought you could do with some provisions here.'

'Thank you,' he replied with delighted surprise, taking them from her.

'There's another ham sandwich too – you know, because I ate half of your other one,' she said.

'You spoil me!' he said humbly. 'Want to come and see my lab?'

Prairie followed Gil down the corridor, the sole of her shoes echoing with each step. *Clack, clack, clack.* Gil stopped at a set of double doors on the right.

'My lab,' he said proudly. 'This is where the magic happens.' He set the groceries down on a bench. Scientific instruments and glass beakers jostled for space on every surface. It was all very clinical.

One wall displayed a picture of Blush Lake taken during a storm, just as a forked bolt of lightning struck the pan and lit up the sky in a tremendous flash. Gil noticed her gaze.

'Petrichor,' he said.

'Pardon?'

'Petrichor. It's what I call that picture.' Seeing Prairie's confusion, he explained. 'It's the smell in the air after a big thunderstorm, when the earth has been washed clean again. Two Australian scientists coined that phrase a couple of years ago. We're famous for naming the smell of rain, *Petrichor!*'

'What does lightning smell like?' asked Prairie.

Gil thought. 'Ozone,' he answered. 'A bit like chlorine bleach. I can smell a storm coming long before it arrives. It's one of my party tricks.'

Prairie smiled despite her mood and studied Gil's handsome face. He was blissfully unaware of the storm clouds gathering, of the impending ozone and petrichor that would soon surround him. She took a deep breath and said, 'Did you find your key?'

'Key? Oh, no,' said Gil, remembering. 'I've no idea where I've put it. It'll turn up. I *hope.* Until then, I'm stuck sleeping in the back there.'

'Was it small and silver?' asked Prairie. 'About this big?' She indicated with her thumb and forefinger.

'Yes,' said Gil, hopefully.

'Was it a skeleton key?'

Gil scratched his head. 'Uh, I'm not sure. Did you find a key?' Prairie nodded.

'That's great,' said Gil. 'Whereabouts?'

'The silo,' said Prairie. She watched Gil's face carefully. 'I found a small silver key out at the silo.' His smile disappeared.

'Wow, that's…okay. Skeleton key, you say?'

'Would I have found a key belonging to you out at the silo, Gil?' Prairie asked softly, dreading the answer.

Gil said nothing. He seemed to be searching for words. His mouth opened and closed like a guppy taking in air.

'Gil,' said Prairie, looking deep into his eyes. 'Why would I have found a key belonging to you at the silo?' And then, 'Have you been out at the silo recently?'

Prairie saw his eyes darken and then glisten as they filled with tears. Gil swallowed and nodded. And there it was. A clap of thunder, a bolt of lightning that shattered the space between them. Ozone. Petrichor.

16

Bush Telegraph

'I thought you'd be in sooner than this, good Constable.' Alan Evans the Elder bustled out from behind the counter. He snipped the lock on the door and flipped the sign. *Closed.*

'Really?' Timms was surprised. 'Why is that, then?'

'The death of that young lass,' said Evans. 'Expect you'll be speaking to the whole town?'

Timms cleared his throat and puffed out his chest. 'Yes,' he said. 'Yes, I am commencing my enquiries with the town. There is a process that needs to be followed. I have been gathering my evidence; fear not.'

The jeweller nodded. 'Right then, should I put the kettle on?'

'Not for me, thanks,' said Timms. He'd had five cups today already. He pulled out his notepad and pen. On the top he'd written:

Alan Evans, Evans & Son (Jeweller): 2.00pm, 21st March 1967

'I understand Miss Lee was a customer of Evans and Son.'

'Yes,' said Evans. 'Somewhat of a regular customer. She bought quite a lot of jewellery from us over the years.'

'When did you last see Miss Lee?'

Evans thought. 'I think it was Tuesday. Hang on.' He went to a cumbersome leather-bound ledger and ran his bony finger down the page. 'Yes, Tuesday morning. About eleven o'clock.'

'Did she buy anything?'

'Yes, she did. She bought a sterling silver bracelet, diamond-encrusted, just like this one.' He pulled a blue velvet pad from a glass display case and presented it to Timms. The string of diamonds sparkled like frost on a windowpane. Timms whistled.

'How much was this item?'

'One hundred and fifty dollars.'

Timms whistled again and scribbled in his pad. 'You said Miss Lee was a regular customer, Mr Evans. What else did she buy – and when?'

'Let's see.' Evans adjusted his glasses on the bridge of his nose and consulted his ledger. 'A nine-carat gold diamond solitaire ring, eighty dollars, on the fifth of March; a pair of pearl earrings, again nine carat gold setting, fifty dollars, on the twelfth of February; a – oh, that piece was quite stunning – a heart-shaped locket with a sapphire inset and box chain, that was eighteen carat, ninety dollars. On the fifteenth of December last year, just before Christmas, so I suppose it was a present. On October, twenty-third – oh, yes, that's right – a string of pearls was purchased – freshwater, cultured, forty dollars – with a marcasite clasp. She brought it back for repair in November. The clasp had been damaged. Quite the job to repair it, I recall.'

Timms' mouth had dropped open. 'That's an extensive list,' he said, wondering how much a telephonist earned at the PMG. 'Anything else?'

Evans flipped back through his ancient ledger and scanned each page. 'Hmmm, a watch, leather band, mother of pearl face, twenty dollars, but that was back in January last year, and before that, can't see anything…'

'So, most of the custom was between October last year and Tuesday? Six months?'

'It appears so.'

'Mr Evans, may I trouble you to go through your ledger and record each purchase Miss Lee made and the date she made it?'

'How far do you want me to go back?' asked Evans, peering over the rims of his glasses.

'When does that ledger start?' asked Timms.

'New Year's Day, Nineteen Sixty-Five.'

'New Year's Day, Nineteen Sixty-Five it is then please, Mr Evans.'

On the footpath outside the jeweller, Timms did some mental arithmetic. *Briar Lee spent four hundred and ten dollars on jewellery in six months. That's an incredible amount of money,* he thought. *I must ask Miss Humble what a telephonist earns.* He hoped the question wouldn't seem too impertinent. This was a murder enquiry, after all.

○   ○   ○

Prairie stood there, stunned.

'I know what you're thinking,' said Gil. 'I –'

'Do you?' snapped Prairie, cutting him off. 'I hardly know what I think myself.'

Gil sighed and sunk into a chair. He put his head in his hands for a few seconds and when he raised it, Prairie noticed just how unwell he looked.

'The night of Heck Johnson's sheep, you and I left the bar and went to the balcony,' he said, looking up.

Prairie nodded. 'Go on.'

Gil took a deep breath. 'After we said goodnight, I went to the bathroom and had a shower. When I came back to the room, a piece of paper had been shoved under my door. It was a note.'

'A note from whom?'

'From you.'

'*Me?*' Prairie stared at him incredulously. 'I never left you a note.'

'I know that – *now*,' said Gil, looking abashed.

'What did it say?'

'It asked me to meet you at the silo at eleven o'clock.'

'What on earth for?'

'It said '*Gil, it's Prairie. Meet me at the silos at eleven o'clock. There's something I want to show you.*"

'What on earth did you think I would want to show you at a grain silo in the middle of the night?' asked Prairie, astonished. Gil blushed but said nothing. Understanding, Prairie felt herself colour too. 'It's absolutely preposterous!' she huffed. 'Didn't you think to knock on my door and ask me?'

'Well, no. I thought maybe…I don't know.' He shifted uncomfortably on the chair.

Prairie softened. 'So, you drove out there?'

'Yes.'

'And?'

'And I waited. Eventually, another car pulled up. It wasn't Baby Blue though. It was Briar in that little red Mini.'

'*Briar* wrote the note?' Prairie gaped. 'What did she want?'

'She wanted to blackmail me.'

'*Blackmail?* Blackmail you about what?'

'Are you going to repeat everything I say?' Gil asked testily.

'Sorry.'

Gil sighed. 'It seems she intercepted a call between me and the Head Office in Melbourne. She understood from that call that Blush Salt was directly responsible for the death of Heck Johnson's sheep. She believed the call was about land acquisition for the salt works and that we had admitted to poisoning the sheep in order to acquire his land. She felt that was proof of what Heck Johnson accused me of in the pub.'

'What did she want?' Prairie cast her mind back to that night-shift. A sick feeling settled in the pit of her stomach.

'She wanted me to pay her to keep quiet about the call. She said that if Heck Johnson and the other farmers became aware of that phone call, then going to the police to admit what I'd done would be preferable to *farm justice.*' She wanted two hundred dollars for her silence.'

'Oh Gil,' said Prairie, sitting down next to him. 'What was the call to Melbourne *really* about? How did she get it so wrong?'

Gil looked agitated. 'This can't be made public, Prairie. Not just yet. The reason I'm here is to assess the potential for creeping salinity in the soil. I've found evidence of it – the salina is making its way west to those properties bordering the salt works – including Heck Johnson's farm. Salt – it's not good for the earth. Nothing but bacterial algae and shrubs like saltbush can grow in it. In a few years, those farms won't produce crops at all, and they won't be able to sustain livestock easily.'

'What did you tell her?'

'I laughed. I told her that she was so far left of field it was ridiculous. But of course, I couldn't tell her what the call was really about. I refused to pay and told her to go to Constable Timms if she was so sure she was right. I got in my car and drove back to the hotel. She was just standing there, stunned. I swear she was alive when I left her, Prairie. You have to believe me.' Gil Sanders looked so defeated that Prairie found that she did.

'We have to go and tell Constable Timms,' she said gently. 'He'll be taking statements from us all anyway. Better we get it over with sooner rather than later.' She thought for a moment. 'Did you happen to notice what Briar was wearing on her feet?'

Gil thought. 'She looked shorter than usual. I suppose she was wearing flat shoes. I didn't notice specifically what she was wearing at all. It was dark and I wanted to get the hell out of there.' He sighed. 'This is going to look so bad for the business, but it's nothing to do with us. It's an effect of the climate, nothing to do with our salt harvesting practices.'

'Come on,' said Prairie. 'Let's go give the good policeman a geology lesson.'

O   O   O

Timms drove his patrol car to Reynolds' Automotive, the last business on Grain Street heading north. He could easily have walked there from Evans & Son. In fact, he could have left his car parked at the station altogether. But he'd done that once before, rather fancying the way English bobbies strolled up and down the streets of London, saying *'Afternoon'* to everyone they met, when a car careened through town taking out a rubbish bin and Battersby's fibreglass dancing pig before hooning away to Brewer's Hill.

Timms had been forced to commandeer Sylvia Hamer's bicycle and chased the perpetrator for half a mile before giving up. That was in the Spring of 1965. He couldn't be certain, but he suspected it might have been a contributing factor to his performance in the Senior Constable's Exam in the Summer of 1966. Since then, he was rarely out of sight of the patrol car.

Jim Reynolds was under the hood of a cream Ford Falcon.

'Sure, I got time to talk about Briar Lee,' he said, without lifting his head from the engine. 'As long as you ask your questions while I work. Say, pass me that socket wrench. No, not that one, the seven-eight inch. Forget it, I'll get it myself.' He emerged from under the bonnet, smeared with grease.

'When did you last see Miss Lee?'

Reynolds wiped his hands on a rag and thought. 'When she picked up her car.'

'That was?'

'Must've been…Tuesday? Let's see. Mini broke down on Monday. Flat battery. She called us and we went out to give her a jump start but the battery was cactus. We towed it back to the shop.'

'Where did the car break down?'

'About a mile and a half out of town. She called us from the exchange. Left the keys in the car and we loaded it, no problem.'

'What time did she collect the car?'

'We did it first thing. It was done by lunchtime. Think she popped in around one?'

'Did she mention anything out of the ordinary?'

'How would I know what wasn't ordinary with that girl?'

Timms stiffened. 'How do you mean?'

'How do *you* mean?'

'I mean…how did she *seem?* Did she say what her plans were? Afterwards?'

Reynolds shrugged. 'Why would she discuss her plans with me? I'm just the mechanic, Mate. She seemed fine.'

'Did she pay upfront?'

'Yep. She paid in cash. No problem.'

'Thanks for your time,' said Timms, putting his notebook and pencil back in his breast pocket. 'I may be in touch again.'

'No worries,' said Reynolds, leaning back into the bonnet. 'Although, you'd be better off talking to my apprentice if you want to know what was and wasn't ordinary about Briar Lee.'

'Where is young Eli?'

'Out fetching a can of Elbow Grease,' said Reynolds casually.

○　○　○

Timms was standing on the pavement beside his patrol car outside the motor shop, looking up and down Grain Street and wondering where to direct his questions next, when Prairie Humble's Morris Minor purred down the street. He waved and was surprised when she pulled in behind his car. The passenger window rolled down, revealing the tall man from the saltworks. Timms was slightly taken aback.

'Hello,' he said gruffly. Prairie leaned forward across the passenger.

'We have to speak to you, Constable,' she said. 'It's very important.'

'You'd best follow me to the station then,' he said. And he climbed into his patrol car and drove exactly one block with Baby Blue close behind.

Jonetta Williams and Sylivia Hamer were on the opposite corner, in front of the Post Office. They stopped mid-conversation and stared, mouths agape as Constable Timms, Prairie and Gil Sanders entered the tiny police station. Prairie's heart sank. *That's all we need,* she thought.

Prairie sat beside Gil, opposite the constable at his desk and listened as Gil recounted his movements the night he saw Briar Lee at the Wheatsheaf silos. Timms scribbled away on a pad and nodded from time to time.

'And what time was it when you left the silo, Mr Sanders?'

Gil thought. 'I can't have been there for more than fifteen minutes. So maybe a quarter past eleven?'

'Eleven-fifteen on Tuesday night. That's the last confirmed sighting of Briar Lee so far.' He put down his pen and rubbed his eyes. 'That makes you the last person to have seen Miss Lee alive, Mr Sanders.'

'No, it doesn't!' Gil protested. 'Surely the person that murdered her was the last person to see her alive. And I can assure you, Constable, that person was not *me.*' Prairie patted Gil's hand instinctively.

'That may be so, Mr Sanders,' said Timms, eyeing the hand-pats with circumspection, 'But until my investigation runs its course, you are now officially a suspect.' He picked up the telephone but there was still no dial tone. 'This damned phone line,' he said, exasperated. 'How much longer, Miss Humble?'

'I'm sure I have no idea,' Prairie replied. Timms looked at the plastic bags on his desk and groped for one.

'Do you recognise this key, Mr Sanders?'

Gil took the plastic bag and examined the small silver skeleton key and shrugged. 'I couldn't say, for sure. I mean, I've misplaced the key to my cabin and that key *is* small and silver, but I've never really paid that much attention to it, since I've never actually used the cabin.'

'Well, there's one way to know for sure,' said Timms. 'If I can ask you both to get into the patrol car?'

Jonetta Williams and Sylivia Hamer were still on the opposite corner when the trio emerged and piled into Timms' vehicle. Jonetta gasped and grabbed Sylivia's arm.

'Look Sylivia,' she breathed. 'They've only gone and arrested him. I knew it was him. Killed the sheep and now he's killed the girl.'

'Bastard,' Sylivia seethed. They watched the car head north out of town and then turned, hurrying as fast as their legs would carry them to the first pair of ears they could find.

O O O

Timms stood with Gil and Prairie at the saltworks cabin door. Prairie was grateful there was nobody else about. They were all busy in the administrative building or out on the pans. Timms took a pair of rubber gloves out of his pocket and opened the plastic bag. He slipped the small key out and examined the lock of the cabin door carefully. Gil and Prairie held their breath as Timms pressed the key to the lock. Prairie almost whooped with joy when he was unable to insert it. Timms straightened.

'Well, Mr Sanders, this appears not to be your key.'

Gil looked glum. 'No,' he said. 'I suppose I really have lost it out on the salt pan.'

'You realise,' said Timms gravely. 'This only proves that this key doesn't fit this lock. By your own admission, you saw Briar Lee at the silo, and unless I can find someone who saw her any time between eleven-fifteen on Tuesday night and the time Sam Swallow found her body on Wednesday night, you remain the prime suspect. By rights, I ought to arrest you.'

'Surely you need more evidence than that?' Prairie pleaded, alarmed.

Timms thought. 'I'd like to search your room.'

'Don't you need a search warrant for that?' asked Gil.

'Well, yes. Yes, I suppose I do. But if you've nothing to hide… It's either that, or I arrest you on suspicion of the murder of Briar Lee. I am at liberty to hold you for twenty-four hours, you know.'

Gil took Timms into the laboratory and allowed him to search through the implements there and through his personal belongings in the little room out the back. *I wonder,* thought Timms, *whether he has 'lost' the key to that cabin on purpose. Could the murder weapon and bloodied clothes be in that room?* He considered coming back with Barry Skipton.

'Please don't leave town, Mr Sanders. I'm sure I'll have further questions for you. I'd rather avoid locking you in the cell at the station, if possible.'

'I'd like to avoid that too,' said Gil, shocked.

O   O   O

Prairie rode with Constable Timms back into town. 'I'm certain Gil didn't do anything wrong,' she said.

'How well do you actually know him?' said Timms. 'Statistically, most murders are committed by people known to the victim, Miss Humble.' Timms had no idea whether that was true or not, but it sounded plausible.

'How have your other lines of enquiry gone?' said Prairie, hoping to divert the constable's attention.

'I have commenced them,' said Timms. 'Tell me, was Briar Lee romantically involved with anyone?'

'She was involved with quite a few, as Olive puts it.'

'Eli Schwartz from Reynolds' Automotive?'

'The apprentice? Yes, Olive did say something about that.'

'I must speak to Miss Wellshorn, sooner rather than later.'

'Well, she's stuck in the exchange with nothing to do right now. I'm sure she'd be happy to give you a statement.'

As they were passing the exchange anyway, Timms pulled off the highway onto Telegraph Road. Olive was grateful for the company and made them tea. Prairie offered to wait outside, but Olive asked her to stay.

'Miss Wellshorn, please forgive my impudence. How much does a telephonist earn each week?'

'It depends on the grade.'

'I'm interested in what Miss Lee would have earned.'

'Ah. Well Briar was on a lower rate than I was, as I'm a senior. And less than Prairie, as a casual. She would have been earning about forty-five dollars a week.'

'Miss Lee spent a rather considerable sum on jewellery,' Timms observed.

'Yes,' said Olive. 'I think she spent rather a lot on all sorts of things.'

'Do we have any idea how Miss Lee may have been able to afford board in town and the normal associated costs of living plus the additional…luxuries?'

'No idea,' said Olive. 'I never really asked her. Prairie and I were discussing that. Her parents are in Golga – maybe they give her an allowance?'

'I understand that Miss Lee was not in a relationship, but may have had a…dalliance? With Eli Schwartz?'

'I know she had dates with a lot of different men over time, but yes, I think she did see Eli more regularly than the others. I don't ever recall her saying that *'so and so bought me this,'* or *'so and so bought me that.'* I rather formed the impression that she bought her clothes, or handbags, or jewellery herself.'

'Was…?' Timms was decidedly uncomfortable. 'That is…'

Prairie and Olive leaned forward. Timms' face turned the colour of a tomato.

'Are you alright, Constable?' asked Olive. 'Can I get you some water?'

'Was Miss Lee…the money. On the side…did she…?'

'Are you asking me whether Briar was *on the game?*' Olive sat back in her chair, dumfounded. Timms looked as though he were about to faint. He shifted from one buttock to the other. Prairie raised her eyebrow. 'You know, I'd never thought of that,' said Olive quietly. 'I suppose anything is possible.'

'You don't seem overly concerned by that, Miss Wellshorn.'

'Should I be?' Olive snapped. 'It's not my business how Briar got her money over and above what she earned here. And she certainly wasn't sleeping with any husband of mine. And I might add at this juncture, that just because Briar went out on dates with lots of different men, it didn't necessarily mean that she was intimate with any of them.'

'Yes, of course,' said Timms, chastened. He scribbled down some notes in his book.

O   O   O

Having exhausted all his questions, Timms offered to drive Prairie back to her car. As soon as they were making their way down Telegraph Road, Prairie turned to the constable.

'There's something I think I need to tell you. I'm not sure that blackmailing Gil was an isolated incident.' She went on to explain to Timms how it was possible to listen in on a call and that she had seen Briar do this on two occasions. 'There are legitimate reasons when a telephonist needs to do this, of course, but Olive confirmed that Briar would never have needed to do this in her role.'

She told Timms about Mabel Wattage being fired and said, 'I can't prove it, but I have an awful feeling that perhaps at some point, Briar listened in on one of Mabel's weekly phone calls to her son. Perhaps Briar tried to blackmail Mabel and when Mabel didn't pay, she tipped Mr Peterson off and got her fired. Although Mabel did seem genuinely not to know how Mr Peterson had become aware of the fact she had a child. What if…what if Briar had been blackmailing other people in the region? Could that be how she got all that money? And what if…what if somebody she was extorting wanted to silence her?'

'It's certainly a possibility,' said Timms. 'How could we prove she was extorting others aside from Mr Sanders? We'd need another victim to come forward.'

'Should we speak to Mabel Wattage, do you think?'

'Worth a try,' said Timms.

'There's something else,' said Prairie. 'That key. We know it doesn't belong to Gil, but it's something that Tom Rizzoli said. He said he locked the exchange door yesterday morning because he supposed Briar had a *'sneaky key.'* Olive asked him why he would think that, but he just shrugged. It's an odd thing to say, don't you think? What if the key we found belonged to Briar? What if it fits the lock of the exchange?'

'I wish you'd said something earlier, Miss Humble,' said Timms, executing a U-turn across the highway and heading back towards the little red building. 'I could have tried the lock then and there.'

O   O   O

As it turned out, the skeleton key did not belong to the exchange door. But the exercise certainly gave Timms food for thought and two new witnesses to question: Mabel Wattage and Tom Rizzoli. On the ride home, it was agreed that Prairie would speak to Mabel first, to smooth the way given the sensitive nature of the enquiries.

As the patrol car neared the police station, Timms and Prairie saw, to their utter dismay, a crowd already gathered outside.

'Oh, this doesn't look good,' Timms murmured. Prairie recognised some of the angry faces from the café and the grocery store. Others too, who drank in the hotel. And amongst them, the smug, fat face of Jonetta Williams. Prairie wanted to slap it.

'Get straight into your car, Miss Humble. I suggest you head back out of town for a bit, until I can calm them down. Can you go back to the exchange?' Prairie nodded dumbly.

Timms pulled up beside Baby Blue and Prairie slid in behind the wheel. As she gunned the engine and made a wide U-turn in the street, she looked in the rear-vision mirror. The mob had surrounded the policeman. *Why am I fleeing like the fugitive?* she thought angrily. She despised the people of Wheatsheaf at that moment.

17
Sorting Wheat from Chaff

'So, have you arrested the bastard, Timms? Where is he?'

'He should be locked up!'

'He's let him go!'

'You're not up to this Timms, weak as piss! Get the Golga squad down here!'

A maelstrom of angry, jeering faces surrounded Timms, barring the way as he tried to push past them to get to the sanctuary of his station.

'Please,' he said, holding up his hands, appealing for calm. 'Enquiries are continuing. Nobody needs to be arrested at this stage.' The plea was met with a collective groan and more vitriol about his level of competency. 'I need you all to calm down and head home. Hey!' A cowpat sailed through the air from the depths of the crowd and knocked his cap off. The jeers turned to laughter.

'Right!' he shouted, bending to retrieve his cap. 'Anyone left on this corner in three seconds will be arrested for breach of peace.' Nobody moved. 'Right!' he yelled again, incensed, 'I'm arresting the lot of you. I know who each and every one of you are, and where you live. And I don't care that you'll all be crammed into one tiny cell.'

The threat got the crowd dispersing enough that he was able to push past into the station. He locked the door behind him and drew the blinds. He collapsed against the desk, panting. He picked up the desk phone, hoping for a dial tone. The silence was deafening.

O   O   O

At the insistence of the constable, Prairie drove north out of town, instead of going back to the hotel, which is all she really wanted to do. The sun would be setting soon. She supposed she could sleep on the little cot in the exchange, although it was likely Olive would stay there at her post, waiting for the lines to be fixed.

She considered heading out to the saltworks – she wanted to see Gil, but that wouldn't be proper. So, she decided to drive out to Blush Lake and wait for darkness to fall. Then she'd head back into town and sneak up to her room in the hotel by the back door, hoping not to encounter anyone on the way.

As she approached the Comfrey homestead, she was surprised to see Agnes Comfrey out the front, chatting to a priest. Prairie recognised Father Childers from the café. Seeing Baby Blue's approach, Agnes waved furiously. Prairie slowed the car.

'Hello, Agnes.'

'Hello, Prairie. Prairie, this is Father Childers – from Our Lady of Perpetual Sorrow. Father, Prairie Humble.'

'Hello, Father.'

'Hello, Miss Humble. I'm pleased to make your acquaintance. Miss Comfrey has been telling me what a comfort you've been to her in this saddest of times.'

'Oh!' Prairie blushed.

'Hopefully, we'll see you at one of our services soon – I assume you observe the faith, of course?'

Prairie smiled. 'I observe *a* faith, Father,' she said sweetly. Father Childers seemed not to mind.

'Splendid. Miss Comfrey, I'll leave you in the hands of your friend now,' (he pronounced the word 'nigh' in his thick, Belfast brogue) 'and be on my way. Don't be a stranger to the Church.' He hopped onto a bicycle and pedalled off.

'I baked a cake,' said Agnes. She appeared to be in brighter spirits today. 'Would you come in for some tea?' Prairie gratefully accepted the offer and drove them both up the long driveway to the homestead.

The house was warm and cosy. Agnes had lit a fire. Table lamps cast a golden glow about the room. It did not seem as gloomy today. Prairie followed Agnes through to the kitchen. A big, old-fashioned range took up a large portion of the wall. The solid oak dining table had been carefully laid with a blue-patterned tablecloth. Next to the dirty teacups was a smattering of old photos.

'Here, let me clear those away,' said Agnes. She touched the white China teapot. 'Tea's gone cold. I'll brew a fresh pot.' Agnes deftly swept away the used crockery. She emptied the tea-pot and rinsed it in the sink. The dresser with the good China was in another room. Agnes went to fetch it.

'I'll put the kettle on,' Prairie called to her, wanting to be useful. She missed having a kitchen and wondered whether Agnes would let her do some baking one day. She picked up the old, blackened kettle and accidentally knocked the handle of a heavy frying pan, equally tarnished. Prairie lunged and caught it before it clattered off the range. She filled the kettle with cold water from the deep farmhouse sink and searched for some matches. She found a packet of *Red-Heads* on top of the range and had lit one just as Agnes came back carrying a fresh stack of cups and plates. Prairie recognised the blue forget-me-knots and smiled.

'I must say, it is nice to have visitors,' said Agnes. 'And two in one day!' She placed the crockery on the table and bustled over to the range. 'Here, shall I do that? You're my guest.' Prairie had already opened the burner and ignited the stream of town gas. Agnes hefted the heavy kettle onto the blue flame.

'What a beautiful kitchen, Agnes,' Prairie mused. 'I do so miss having a kitchen.'

'You must be tired of take-away sandwiches and pub dinners,' Agnes observed. She went to the fridge and produced a Victoria sponge, beautifully decorated with fresh cream and strawberries and lovingly dusted with the finest coating of icing sugar. Agnes and the priest had already devoured a quarter of the cake. 'I'm having seconds,' said Agnes. 'No use watching my weight.' Agnes was as thin as a rake, but wiry, with strong limbs. No doubt, Prairie mused, from the austere conditions she grew up with.

'Mother never approved of fanciful baking,' she said. 'I cannot remember us ever using the good China. And now I've used it three times in one week!' Prairie smiled at the woman's ability to be upbeat despite her circumstances. Agnes cut an enormous slice of cake and handed a plate to Prairie.

'Goodness,' said Prairie. 'I won't eat my dinner.' That was a point. Dinner would be well and truly over by the time she dared to venture back to the hotel. She decided that if Agnes offered her seconds, she'd accept.

While they waited for the kettle to boil, Prairie tuned her attention to the photographs by her right hand. Agnes noticed and picked one up. She gazed at it lovingly before handing it to Prairie. It was a serious portrait of a man and a woman, the man seated and the woman standing at his side, her hand on his shoulder. Prairie turned the picture over – '*1918*' was written in the neatest of copperplate in faded ink.

'My parents were married just after the war,' said Agnes, sorting another photograph from the pile, a wedding picture, and handing it to Prairie. The couple in the wedding photograph looked just as grim as they had done in the portrait. 'I was thinking it might be nice to put one in a frame and have it on the casket, during the service. I thought it might be nice to have some hydrangeas too, but it's not the season for them.' She gazed sadly out of the kitchen window. 'Mother did like the hydrangeas here,' she said. 'You should see the garden in Summer, Prairie. It's wonderful. The roses and the hydrangeas. It's just dead now, like everything else.' Agnes suddenly looked so sad.

The kettle began to whistle on the stove. Agnes jumped up to make the tea. Prairie carefully placed the wedding photograph on the pile and picked up another. It was a picture of a man, undoubtedly Agnes' father, holding a little girl aloft in a field of wheat. The little girl was laughing, clearly having the time of her life. Prairie flipped the picture – *'1923'*.

'Is this you, Agnes?'

Agnes turned, smiling. 'Yes. That's me and my father. I was six years old in that picture. He took me to work with him a lot.' She poured scalding water on leaves in the teapot. The aroma of brewing tea filled the kitchen. 'I miss him. It makes me happy to think that he and Mother are together again. She was never really the same after he died.' Agnes brought the pot to the table and poured out two cups. She handed one to Prairie. 'How's the cake?'

Prairie carved a large piece with her fork. It was the softest sponge she'd ever tasted with just the right balance of sweetness. 'This is delicious, Agnes,' she said. They ate in silence.

Eventually, Agnes said 'I hope I haven't kept you from your work.'

Prairie shook her head and swallowed another piece of cake. 'Lines are still down,' she said.

'Oh!' said Agnes, surprised.

'Truth is,' said Prairie, 'I didn't really have anywhere to go.' And she told Agnes about the townsfolk blaming Gil for the murder of Briar Lee. She was careful to leave out some of the details but told Agnes enough for her to realise that she wasn't safe going back to the hotel just yet.

'You do right to stay away for now,' said Agnes. 'The people in this town can be so spiteful. We've had all sorts of bother over the years. And your poor friend's car! Imagine if you left your dear little motor out in the street? Goodness knows what someone might take it into their head to do.' Prairie nodded glumly.

'Well, I was just going to make myself some bacon and eggs for dinner,' said Agnes. 'I do like bacon and eggs. I'd happily have them for my breakfast and my tea. We've been a bit naughty, I suppose, having our dessert before our tea. Let me cook you some bacon and eggs – and then we can have a second dessert! You are most welcome to stay here as long as you like. I could even make up a bed in the spare room!'

'I don't want to put you out,' Prairie began to protest.

'Not at all,' said Agnes. She was already on her way to the refrigerator to take out a pound of sliced bacon. 'The company helps me not to dwell on things.' Agnes insisted on Prairie resting, so Prairie sat in the warm little kitchen and basked in the delicious smell of frying bacon.

O   O   O

The alarm clock rang shrilly at six o'clock on Friday morning. Timms started violently and flung out a hand to silence the beast. He groaned. He'd passed a fitful night, up at every sound, peaking out through the blinds and satisfying himself that both doors to the station were firmly locked before crawling back into bed. He judged that he'd had less than three hours sleep by the time the alarm clock rudely announced the start of the working day.

Timms sighed. He laid there, staring at the ceiling and uttered a silent prayer that he would find the telephone lines repaired when he picked up the heavy Bakelite receiver that morning. He was completely out of his depth and needed help. As much as he loved the company of Prairie Humble, her sweet smile and the scent of her hairspray, the anger of the town worried him. He was used to dealing with the dissatisfaction of one or two of the townsfolk – they often took umbrage at a request from him to do this or that, or to refrain from doing this or that – but a mob was something entirely different and he worried that he would ulti-mately find himself bundled into the back of a farm utility vehicle and taken out to a field to be shot. He shuddered.

He washed and then shaved, trimming his moustache metic-ulously around his top lip. As he slapped his face with a cologne that made his eyes water, he formed a plan of action for the day. Dressing, he tightened his Windsor knot a little too forcefully and almost choked himself. He loosened the cravat's grip and took a deep breath. He stared into the mirror, searching the doleful dark eyes that stared back at him. *Emmanuel,* he said to himself, *you have absolutely no idea what you are doing. But keep going, Son. Keep going.* The mantra, intoned in the voice of the father he never really knew, was something he repeated often.

At precisely eight-thirty, he left the station by the back door, having first made sure neither Jonetta Williams nor Sylvia Hamer were lurking about, got into his patrol car and headed for Reynolds' Automotive.

'I take it Eli hasn't been sent off for a left-handed spanner,' said Timms in a tone that he hoped conveyed he was in no mood for nonsense. Jim Reynolds smirked and jerked his head.

'He's out the back, washing an auto we finished last night. Go through.'

Timms walked to the rear of the workshop and through a door that led to a yard. Several automobiles sat in various stages of disrepair. Eli Schwartz was half-heartedly washing a cream Volkswagen that Timms recognised as belonging to Father Childers. Eli was sloshing more water on himself and the ground than was getting near the car. He jumped at Timms approach.

'Figured you'd be wanting to talk to me,' he said quietly, throwing the sponge into the bucket. Unexpectedly, Timms found Eli Schwartz cooperative, almost eager to talk.

'I've known Briar most of my life,' he said. 'She was a year above me at school, although she left when she was fourteen. Folks moved to Golga. Didn't think I'd ever see her again. But she came back three years ago. She'd changed – a lot. I hardly recognised her.'

'You went out together?' Eli nodded.

'For a while. About six months. Then it was on and off for the rest of the time.'

'On and off?' asked Timms. He didn't understand how a relationship could be on and then off. Either it was or it wasn't, surely?

'I wanted to get engaged,' he said. 'I bought a ring and everything. I proposed, but she turned me down. She said I should finish my apprenticeship first, but I've only got six months to go now, so I asked again. She said didn't want to be tied down. She wanted to travel. I said, *'Fair enough.'* But the thing is, for all her talk of travel, she never actually went anywhere, except to Golga. I guess what she meant was that she just didn't want to be with me.'

'That must have been a bit upsetting for you, Eli?' Timms knew it was a leading question, and he wasn't surprised when the apprentice's eyes narrowed, and his jaw tightened. But Eli just shrugged.

'When was it that you last asked her to marry you?' asked Timms.

'On Tuesday afternoon. She had a day off and came in to collect her car.'

O   O   O

Despite Thursday's challenges, Prairie slept soundly in Agnes Comfrey's spare bed. When she awoke, a shaft of sunlight streaked the pale blue counterpane through a chink in the curtains. She could hear Agnes up already, bustling about in the kitchen. She dressed quickly and wandered out. Agnes was at the range in her apron, ancient frying pan in hand, ready to fry up another batch of bacon.

'Good morning,' Agnes greeted her. 'I hope you slept well?'

'I did indeed,' said Prairie, hugging herself. It was chilly in the kitchen. 'In fact, I think it was the best sleep I've had the whole time I've been in Wheatsheaf.'

Agnes beamed proudly. 'Perhaps I should turn my home into a *'Bed and Breakfast.'* Bacon and eggs – or something lighter?'

Prairie opted for the lighter choice – a bowl of cornflakes and a cup of coffee. As delicious as it was last night, she didn't want to make the greasy meal a habit. They chatted pleasantly throughout breakfast. Agnes hoped the telephone lines would soon be up. She wanted to be able to move ahead with plans for the funeral. Prairie lifted the heavy Bakelite receiver and confirmed there was still no dial tone.

'Maybe later today?' she said hopefully. 'There must have been some frightful damage for it to have taken this long.'

They discussed their plans for the day. Agnes had promised to wander up to the church to help sort some jumble for the upcoming Autumn Fete. Father Childers thought it was an excellent way of helping Agnes reintegrate into town life following the death of her mother. The ladies who ran the church op-shop were not Jonetta Williams or Sylvia Hamer. Father Childers had asked them to be kind.

Prairie would go back to the Harvest Hotel, bathe and change. She wanted to see Constable Timms, Olive and Gil – although not necessarily in that order.

○　○　○

Mabel Wattage would be a delicate matter. Timms decided she was a potential witness that could wait until after he'd spoken to Prairie. He hadn't seen Mabel around town and wondered if she'd gone to be with her son in Golga.

Tom Rizzoli lived with his parents in a weatherboard house with a wrap-around porch on a street that swept upwards from the main road. The front porch looked down upon the town. Tom's mother was a teacher at the local primary school. His father worked for Blush Salt.

'Tom, you worked with Miss Lee, so I'd just like to ask you some questions about her,' Timms began.

Tom shrugged. 'Sure. But I didn't do it.'

'I'm not suggesting for one minute that you did,' said Timms evenly. 'But I do need to ask questions of the people who knew Miss Lee best. And you did work with her for some time, yes?'

Tom shrugged again. 'We worked some night shifts together.'

'When was the last time you saw Miss Lee?'

Tom thought. 'Monday night. She was on the six-to-midnight shift. I came on at ten o'clock.'

'You spent two hours with Miss Lee?' Tom nodded. 'How did she seem?'

'Her usual self,' said Tom. He held his mouth down at the corners, disinterested.

'What do you mean by *usual self,* Tom?' Tom shrugged.

'I don't know. Briar was…Briar.'

Timms was getting exasperated. 'What did you talk about?'

Tom shrugged again. 'We never really talked much about anything. *If* she talked, it was all about herself, or something she saw in one of the magazines she was endlessly reading. I try not to pay much attention to her. That's what she always wants – for people to pay attention to her. I find her – *found* her, to be irritating, if I'm honest. I generally read on the night shift myself, when I'm not taking calls. The nights are usually pretty quiet.'

Timms was careful with the next question. 'It's possible to listen in on calls, isn't it, Tom?'

Tom nodded. Timms went on.

'But you wouldn't need to do that, unless you were checking the lines or specifically auditing a call. As an overseer? Is that correct?' Tom nodded again. 'Did Briar ever work as an overseer?'

Tom laughed. 'As if Peterson would trust her to do *that!*'

'Is that a *'no'*?'

'No. She was never an overseer or a monitor. She was just a switchie.'

Timms frowned. 'Tom, to your knowledge, did Briar ever listen in on telephone calls?'

Tom scoffed but the answer was unexpected. 'All the time. That's how she spent most of the night shifts. When she wasn't giving herself free telephone calls.'

'Did she ever tell you about the calls afterwards?'

'Sometimes. But not always.'

'Yet you could tell when she was listening in?'

Tom nodded. 'When the switchboard key is pushed forward, the line is being listened to. You only have to look at the position of the key on the switch, which is easy when we're sitting side by side.'

'When we came looking for Miss Lee on Wednesday, you said you were surprised she didn't have a *'sneaky key'* to the exchange. Can you tell me what you meant by that, Tom?' Tom looked uncomfortable. 'It's alright, Tom,' said Timms. 'You aren't in any trouble. But someone has committed a murder in our town, and I need to do all I can to figure out why Miss Lee died – and who killed her. Any piece of information, no matter how trivial or unconnected it may seem, might help me to build a picture of what might have happened.' He wished Prairie was here. She was so much better at cajoling people. He himself felt clumsy and insincere.

Tom sighed and his shoulders dropped, as though he were a deflating balloon. 'I assumed that Olive would have given Briar her own key to the exchange.'

'Why would she do that, Tom?'

The expression on Tom's face was pained. 'This isn't going to get back to Olive or Peterson, is it?'

'If what you end up telling me is connected to the case in any way, I can't make promises. But I do promise that if they don't need to know, they won't hear it from me. That's the best I can do.'

Tom exhaled. 'Olive and Briar were…close.'

'Close? As in good friends?'

'*Very* good friends,' said Tom and shifted uncomfortably. Timms looked at him quizzically. Tom rolled his eyes. 'They were together – *alone* – for part of every single shift they did, except for the two consecutive days when they each had a day off.'

Timms continued to stare dumbly. Tom sighed in exasperation.

'You're not going to make me spell it out, are you?'

18

Water

Our Lady of Perpetual Sorrow stood at the crest of a steep hill overlooking the town. As soon as Prairie dropped Agnes off for a day sorting jumble, she made a beeline for the police station. She found the patrol car gone and the door locked. She carried on to the Harvest Hotel, keeping a weather-eye out for both the constable and any signs of an unruly mob. She particularly kept her eyes peeled for Jonetta Williams and Sylvia Hamer, but fortunately both were occupied with activities elsewhere this morning.

Prairie parked Baby Blue in the gravel yard behind the hotel. Arthur and Stan Banbury were in the yard with a man she didn't recognise, and they all turned to stare as she got out.

'Morning,' said Arthur. 'Felice'll be relieved to see you, love. She worried about you all night.'

'I'm sorry, Arthur,' said Prairie, and then wondered why she was apologising for being a hotel guest that had licence to come and go as she pleased. But she felt compelled to provide an excuse for her overnight absence so added, 'Constable Timms thought I should avoid the area until the mob dispersed. Agnes Comfrey was kind enough to put me up for the night.' Arthur nodded dismissively and returned his attention to the men.

Entering the hotel via the back door, Prairie encountered Felice lugging a vacuum cleaner down the stairs.

'Oh, Pet!' Felice exclaimed. 'Am I overjoyed to see you? I was *so* worried. All *night*, I worried. I says to Arthur, *'Arthur'* I says, *'I'm worried. Get the car out and go look for Miss Humble.'* It's clearly not safe for young ladies out there what with this homicidal maniac all over the place!' She drew a breath and in conspiratorial tones confided 'I don't believe for one minute that lovely Mr Sanders had *anything* to do with it. But you can't tell *them* that!' Felice jerked her head towards Grain Street.

Prairie was forced to explain herself all over again. She thought she detected a shade of disappointment when Felice explained she was not with Gil, but with Agnes Comfrey.

'Never mind, Pet,' said Felice, tapping Prairie's shoulder comfortingly with her scarlet-tipped hand. 'We won't be tolerating *any* nonsense in here. Dr Ted is in Wheatsheaf now, better late than never.' She rolled her eyes, her azure-powdered lids retreating upwards like French awnings. 'He forded the river up at bloody Woop-Woop,' she said, referring to Dumbogan, 'but he's going to take that *disgusting* sheep away. He'll be able to tell the town Gil didn't poison no sheeps.'

Prairie smiled gratefully. *I wish Dr Ted would be able to tell the town that Gil didn't murder Briar Lee,* she thought. That was the more pressing issue. Wearily, Prairie climbed the stairs to bathe and change her clothes.

O O O

Cleansed and fortified, she headed back out to the yard. The three men stood over the sheep.

'Don't come any closer, love,' said Arthur protectively. 'This is grim work.'

No grimmer than identifying a dead body, thought Prairie, but she kept her distance.

'I'd say this sheep was dehydrated,' said the vet thoughtfully. 'It's certainly showing signs of dehydration. Look at that white crust around its mouth. And in the nostrils.'

'Could it be poison?' Arthur asked. Ted ran a hand thoughtfully across his chin.

'It's possible. I'm going to take some samples to test in the lab. I'd like to take a look at Heck Johnson's field too.'

'Instead of samples, can you take the whole damn carcass?' Arthur asked, exasperated. Ted patted him soothingly on the arm.

'Of course, Arthur. Of course. And you can stand me a pint next time I'm in.' He winked and Arthur guffawed.

Prairie slipped behind the wheel of Baby Blue and headed out again, this time towards the exchange, expecting to pass the patrol car at any moment. Timms was nowhere to be seen. She turned into Telegraph Road and parked next to Olive's car. The door to the exchange was open – Olive was no doubt letting some air into the stuffy little building.

Prairie was surprised to find the exchange empty, the switchboards dark and silent. Prairie was about to call out when she heard quiet sobbing.

'Olive?'

A tap ran in the little restroom and Olive appeared. Prairie had obviously surprised her. She was flushed and her eyes were red-rimmed. She'd tried to compose herself by splashing her face with water, but Prairie could easily see that she'd been crying.

'No news on the lines yet, but they must be getting close,' Olive said, smoothing her hair and sniffing.

'Olive dear, whatever is the matter? Are you alright?'

Olive brushed aside Prairie's concern. 'I'm fine. Tea? Was just about to brew a cup.'

'Go on then,' said Prairie, feigning cheerfulness. 'Did you stay here all night?'

'Yes,' said Olive. 'I'd love to go home and bathe. Change my clothes. Would you hold the fort while I do that?'

'Of course.' Prairie watched Olive fill the kettle with hands that trembled slightly. 'Have you eaten anything?' Olive shook her head.

'I had a couple of biscuits. I'm not that hungry.' She reached for a mug – Briar's rose-painted cup, but the cup slipped through her grasp and fell to the floor. It hit the linoleum and shattered into pieces. Olive cried out and clasped her hands to her face. Prairie watched that face crumple and dissolve into tears. 'I'm so stupid!' she gasped.

Prairie stooped to pick up the pieces. 'Of course, you're not, Olive, dear,' she said, soothingly. She was about to drop the shards into the rubbish bin when Olive grabbed her wrist.

'No. Don't do that. Please. I...I'll see if I can glue it back together.'

'Oh Olive, love, why...?' Prairie laughed lightly but the look of consternation on Olive's face stopped her short. Olive's dark eyes were damp and shone with a mix of...what? Grief? Olive looked away.

'Oh Olive, dear,' said Prairie, gently this time. She held out her arms and embraced the woman. 'I'm so sorry.' Olive went limp and sobbed for a moment, finally gathering herself in one long sniff. She pushed the tears off her cheeks. 'I didn't realise...' Prairie began, not really knowing how to continue. She didn't have to. Olive straightened and smoothed her hair.

'I'm just being silly. No fool like an old fool.' Prairie waited quietly for Olive to go on. 'Briar was a handful at times. I'm well aware she used to listen in on calls at night. No matter how many times I told her to be careful...' Olive shook her head, sadly. 'But... she could also be very sweet. That's what I'll choose to remember.'

'You think,' Prairie began carefully, 'You think perhaps Briar overheard something? Something she shouldn't have?'

Olive shrugged. 'What other explanation is there?' she said, matter-of-factly and held out her hand for the sharp pieces of rose-painted porcelain. Prairie handed them to her carefully, and Olive wrapped them gently in her head scarf. 'I'll be as quick as I can,' she said, gathering her coat and handbag.

'Take your time,' said Prairie, and meant it. Olive smiled gratefully and pulled the exchange door open. She paused and turned back.

'Thank you, Prairie,' she said. 'You are remarkably kind,' and then she stepped out into the cool morning air.

○ ○ ○

Hector Johnson's back paddock sloped down towards a remote corner of scrubland.

'This is where you kept the flock, Heck?' Dr Ted Thurgood held his right hand up to his forehead like a visor, shielding his eyes, as he surveyed the surrounding farmland.

'Yep.' Heck snorted deeply and spat. 'Other pastures are fallow. Got to rotate 'em, let 'em recover. Flock's been here since the winter – all twenny of 'em. No problem afore now. I've grazed a flock here every six years since nineteen hunnerd and twenny-three.'

'That's forty-four years,' said Dr Ted, calculating quickly in his head.

'Yep,' Heck intoned, a little defiantly, the vet thought.

Ted Thurgood had been to the Johnson farm many times. He was here at least once every lambing season for some issue or another, but he'd never stood in this field. He looked down the slope. Blush Lake peeped, pink and pale, above the scrub.

'Where did you water the sheep, Heck?' the veterinarian asked.

'Over here.' The farmer waded through the yellowing grass in black rubber boots that looked too big for his bronze, stick-like legs. At seventy-two years of age, Hector Johnson's thoracic spine curved like a bow, but he moved with alacrity, brushing aside golden spears as though he were skating on ice. Ted had to move briskly to keep up.

Heck stopped and stared down at a standpipe jutting up from the earth. It dribbled, incontinent, into the grass. An overturned trough lay discarded nearby. 'I tipped that shit out when the ewe died,' Heck offered, by way of explanation. 'Didn't want the others getting sick, but it was too late. Maybe I should have kept a sample of the poison for you.' His slate-grey eyes looked regretful for a moment.

Ted squatted and held a small glass jar beneath the standpipe and watched the liquid trickle in. It was cloudy and slightly viscous. He held it up, looking at the contents against the sky as if he were appraising a glass of wine. He dipped his right pinky finger into the fluid and cautiously touched it to his tongue. A sharp tang curled his buds. Ted grimaced.

'Bloody hell, Heck! This water is sodium-heavy. It tastes like the Dead Sea! I have an analysis kit in the ute, but I'd say your sheep may as well have been drinking down there at the lake!'

'What are you saying?' asked Heck Johnson, his heavy lids blinking as quickly as the sagging weight of skin would allow.

'*Salt!*' said the veterinarian. 'I'm saying that the standpipe is drawing salty groundwater.'

'See!' thundered Heck at the revelation. 'Those salt bastards *have* poisoned my sheep!'

Realising his mistake, Ted Thurgood rose. 'No, Heck,' he said, soothingly and placed a comforting hand on the farmer's left shoulder. 'We need further testing, of course. I'll conduct an autopsy on your sheep. But, if my suspicions are correct, the water table here is saline. Nobody did this, Heck. This is Mother Nature.'

19

Locks

No *matter how many times I told her to be careful…*

Olive's words came back to Prairie as she sat there, staring at the silent switchboards. Briar had connected a call from Gil Sanders to his boss in Melbourne on Monday night, had slid the switch key upwards, opened the line and had listened in. From that call, Briar had determined that Blush Salt was looking to acquire land and had poisoned Hector Johnson's sheep in order to do so. Briar had then left a note on Tuesday night, masquerading as Prairie, to draw Gil to the silos for one purpose. Blackmail. This, Prairie knew for a fact.

In the quiet telephone exchange, with only the ticking of the wall clock for company, Prairie reflected that she didn't really know Gil Sanders at all. But she felt sure that his gentle energy would never be capable of such unspeakable violence. Somebody had grabbed Briar Lee from behind and had severed her throat with an unimaginable ferocity. Prairie shuddered, got up and made sure the door to the exchange was locked.

Listening in on Gil's call was not an isolated instance – Olive had confirmed that. So, what did Briar know about whom? Prairie was struck with an idea. She went to the pigeonholes at Olive's desk and pulled out the dockets bundled there for the week leading up to Briar's death. Being careful not to mix them up, she sorted through them until she came to Briar's neat cursive script. She took a pad and made a list of all the calls Briar connected on the night before her murder. Her heart beat a little faster when she saw the docket from Blush Salt Works to Melbourne, a trunk-call placed on Monday night at eight-thirty in the evening, a call lasting thirteen minutes.

Most of the eavesdropping likely occurred during the quieter nightshifts, when there was not so much background noise from the other switch operator taking and connecting calls. To listen in undetected by either party required near-perfect silence, lest the listener be discovered. Prairie flicked through the shift roster, noting the dates of the late shifts worked by Briar, or shifts when Briar and Olive worked together. With lack of anything better to do, Prairie located the corresponding bundles of dockets and listed those calls likewise.

On Sunday evening, at seven o'clock, Briar had connected a call from Mabel Wattage to Golga, presumably a call to Mabel's son, Eamon. Had Briar listened in on these calls and discovered Mabel's secret? Had Briar tried to extort Mabel? Did Mabel refuse? Had Briar then tipped off Mr Peterson to get Mabel fired in retaliation? Had Mabel then followed Briar to the silo and slit her throat like a Spring lamb?

I'm being preposterous, Prairie thought, but she kept going and by the time she heard the crunch of tyres on the gravel outside, she had a list of names and numbers going back two months. It was Constable Timms' patrol car. Prairie sighed with relief and let him in.

'I've spoken with Eli Schwartz and Tom Rizzoli this morning,' said Timms, gratefully accepting Prairie's offer of tea.

'Anything of note?'

Timms looked uncomfortable. 'I may need to speak with Miss Wellshorn again. Tom Rizzoli indicated…that is to say he… intimated…ah…they, Miss Wellshorn and Miss Lee…' He crossed and uncrossed each leg.

'Were romantically involved?' Prairie finished for him as she put a teabag into a cup.

Timms stared at her aghast. His face blushed crimson to the roots of his hair. 'I don't know what to say.'

Prairie shrugged. 'It happens. We shouldn't judge. I'm sure you'll handle the matter sensitively. Olive was very upset when I came here this morning. Briar's death has affected her more deeply than I realised. She should be back soon, though.'

Timms shifted uncomfortably. 'I'm sure questioning Miss Wellshorn can wait a bit longer. I'm curious to follow up on the Mabel Wattage lead. Have you spoken with her at all?' he said, quick to change the subject.

'I haven't seen her,' Prairie confessed, shaking her head. 'I think she may have gone back to Golga. That would make sense, given the situation. Dr Ted was at the hotel this morning though, poking about with Hector Johnson's sheep.'

'Ah! Good. We might have a definitive answer there soon, at least.' Prairie handed him a steaming cup. 'Thank you, Miss Humble. Tea is good for the soul.'

'I prefer gin,' Prairie mused.

'Mother's Ruin,' Timms reflected.

'Luckily I am nobody's mother,' Prairie murmured. 'I've been going through the dockets,' she said, nodding towards the list on the table, 'and I've made a note of all the calls Briar connected during her night shifts for the past two months.'

'Excellent,' said Timms. 'Anything stand out?'

'Well, calls from Gil and Mabel Wattage are there, but really, she could have heard any sort of gossip from any of those numbers. There are calls from the police station in there too,' she added, sipping her tea. Timms almost choked on his. As he brushed liquid from his lapel, Prairie said, 'I went back to the silo yesterday. With everything that's happened, I forgot to tell you about it.' Timms plonked his cup on the saucer with gusto and stared.

'I was very careful,' said Prairie earnestly. 'I didn't touch anything. But something occurred to me. The grain shed is padlocked. And there is a door in the utility room that is padlocked too. At first, I thought we should cut the locks with bolt cutters, but then I got to thinking – what if the skeleton key fits one of the locks? Do you think we should check it out?'

The idea appealed to Timms more than questioning Olive Wellshorn about her sexuality, and Mabel Wattage about her parental status. He was eager to buy himself time to work up to those difficult conversations.

When Olive returned to the exchange and relieved Prairie, Timms doffed his cap stiffly, mumbled *'Miss Wellshorn,'* and tried not to make eye contact.

Idiot, thought Olive, as she closed the door behind them.

○ ○ ○

In daylight, and in the company of the policeman, the silos did not seem quite so foreboding. Still, Prairie did her best to avoid looking at *that* spot on the side of the road. They trudged over to the long, triangular grain store.

'I tried to take a look in here,' she said, 'but there are no windows to speak of. And it was too dark to see anything through the cracks in the timber. What's normally in there, anyway?'

'Excess grain from the fields usually,' said Timms. 'It's very busy here during the harvest. You wouldn't think to look at it now.'

They were standing by a pair of sliding doors, fastened by bolt and padlock. Wearing a pair of gloves, Timms took the silver key out of its envelope with one hand and fingered the lock with the other.

'Well, here goes, Monsieur Poirot.'

Prairie held her breath. When the key rotated a quarter-turn in the lock and the clasp yielded with a soft click, Prairie hardly dared to believe her eyes. She stared, dumbly at the lock and then up at Timms. Timms looked equally astonished.

'Well, I didn't expect that,' he breathed quietly.

'What now?' whispered Prairie. 'What if there's someone inside?'

'I hadn't thought of that,' said Timms. 'But if there is, I'd expect they be relieved to see us.'

'Of course,' said Prairie. 'How silly of me.'

Timms put the key along with the padlock in his pocket and brought forth a heavy torch. He held it aloft and, with some exercise of force, pushed the stiff shed door aside. The torch beam cut through the gloom, startling roosting pigeons. The shed was long and mostly empty. Timms pushed aside the other half of the door to let in more light.

'Stay close, Miss Humble,' he said. 'If there is evidence here, we must be careful not to destroy it.' Inching forward, Timms in the lead and Prairie close behind, he swept the torch in a wide arc before him. He scoured the ground for evidence: signs of a struggle, blood, a likely weapon, Briar Lee's left ballet shoe. But there was nothing. The long building had not been disturbed since the harvest – or possibly long before that. Prairie was dejected.

'I was so sure we'd find something in here,' she said. 'How strange that this key fits that lock, though.'

'Not at all,' said Timms. 'That's what a skeleton key is for. This key probably opens a hundred padlocks on fifty different farms around here.'

Prairie helped Timms slide the shed doors shut and watched him reattach the padlock. 'I suppose I should really take this with me,' he said, on second thoughts. 'You didn't touch it, did you Miss Humble? When you were here? I might be able to dust it for fingerprints.'

'Oh!' said Prairie. 'Have you got a finger-print dusting kit at the station?'

'No,' said Timms glumly. 'They don't give me anything like that. That's another job for the coroner and crime lab in Golga.' He pulled a plastic bag out of his trouser pocket, unclasped the lock and dropped it in.

They moved across the silo yard to the small outbuilding in the shadow of the smaller cylindrical cone. Prairie shuddered, thinking of the feral cat on the night they discovered Briar's body. Constable Timms yanked open the door.

'What is this building for?' she asked, as cautiously, they peered in.

'This building gives access to the grain pit and the internal workings of the silo,' Timms replied. 'When the wheat is harvested and threshed, the farmer brings his grain to the silo in his truck.

The trucks marshal over there,' he said, pointing to a hard-standing area. 'Someone from the Golden Grain Company comes along with a probe and takes a sample. See that little kiosk over there? That's where the action happens. The sample of grain is inspected and classified – for size, shape, weight. This determines the overall quality of the grain and how much Golden Grain is willing to pay the farmer for his load.'

Prairie had never thought much about where her bread came from. Timms continued.

'The truck full of grain drives onto the weighbridge over there' (again with a pointed finger) 'and by deducting the weight of the truck before it was filled with grain, the weight of the harvest is calculated. The truck then tips the grain down through that grate. Beneath us, there is a huge underground store – the grain pit. Granary workers go down in there to fumigate the grain. The crops come with all sorts of pests, you know, and we don't want them spoiling the whole stockpile, do we? People are depending on this grain to be milled into flour, after all. No harvest, no bread and other delicious things. That's why we must always be careful going into these silos. We could asphyxiate in the grain or be poisoned by the chemicals used in the fumigation process.' Prairie was suddenly not so keen to be inside the little room.

'Once the grain sits for a while and the granary workers are sure any pests are dead, the grain is moved by a conveyor and bucket elevator up into the silos and stored there until needed for the mill. There are chutes on the other side of this building, near the train tracks. Trucks or cars pulled by a locomotive will line up to be filled through that chute. That's primarily what Sam Swallow does,' said Timms as an aside. 'He takes the grain from all over the silos in this region to the Amity Flour Mill out near Dumbogan.'

'Fascinating,' said Prairie, and she meant it. 'Shall we see if our key fits that padlock?'

'Of course,' said Timms, suddenly remembering why they were standing in the little room. He moved past the jerrycans and, with his gloved hands, examined the padlock. It looked very similar, although not identical to the lock on the grain shed door. He brought the skeleton key out of his pocket, slipped it into the lock and turned it. The clasp resisted at first but soon snapped open. Prairie gasped. Timms brought another plastic bag from his pocket and slipped the second padlock in. 'I hope I remember which is which,' he said.

'Perhaps tear a piece out of your notebook and slip it into the plastic bag with the details of the building you've taken each lock from?' Prairie suggested.

'Excellent idea,' said Timms. 'We'll make a police constable out of you yet!' When he'd done that, he opened the door. His torch beam illuminated the underground storage cavity. A ladder was fixed to the wall beneath the door and led down into the bunker.

'Do you think it's safe to enter?' Prairie asked.

Timms sniffed the air cautiously. 'It doesn't smell too bad,' he said. 'At least not as though someone has just sprayed the area with a fungicide.' He swept the torch beam back and forth. 'There's a little grain left in here, but nothing we'll drown in. I'm happy to go down alone, Miss Humble, if you'd rather stay up here?'

'I certainly would *not* rather stay up here alone, Constable,' Prairie retorted. She now wished others had come with them. She did not relish the idea of being up in that room alone should Briar Lee's killer return to the scene of his crime any more than the idea of being locked in that dark bunker should something happen to the door. But at least down in the pit with Timms, she would not be alone. She dragged a heavy jerry-can, filled with some unknown liquid, across to the bunker door and wedged it open.

'Let me go first then,' said Timms, 'in case the ladder isn't safe.' Gripping the torch firmly in one hand, he descended backwards down the ladder. When he reached the bottom, he called, 'All clear!' and shone the beam so Prairie could see her footing.

Once on the floor, Timms swept the torch in an arc of light, illuminating dark corners. Mice scurried for the shadows. Prairie shuddered. They could see the room was long and rectangular, and the floor littered with traces of grain that failed to make it up into the silos via the grain elevator. It was otherwise devoid of object and – aside from the mice – movement. At the furthest corner of the pit to their right, shafts of light spilled into the gloom from above.

'That area is directly below the grate,' said Timms, and gravitated towards the light like a navy-blue moth, the left-over grain crunching beneath his shoes. Prairie hurried after him.

When they reached the section beneath the grate, Timms swept his torch over the scene. The beam came to rest on an object, inert, on the shallow carpet of grain. Moving closer, they saw it was a pink ballet slipper. Briar Lee's left shoe. Prairie gasped. Spreading out on the surface of the grain, away from the slipper, was a dark stain.

'What is that?' said Prairie, her hands pressed to her lips in revulsion. Timms squatted down and shone his light brightly onto the grain.

'I'd say this is blood,' he said grimly and played the beam upwards to the grate above them. 'This would help to explain why we didn't find any traces of blood up there. I think we have found the execution spot of Briar Lee, Miss Humble.'

20

Reconnection

A wave of nausea swept over Prairie, but she was determined not to be sick. Not down here, not in front of Emmanuel Timms. She prised her eyes from the dark patch of grain and said, 'I need some air.'

'Of course,' said Timms and directed the beam of light back towards the ladder for her. 'I'll come with you.'

'I shall be quite alright,' Prairie assured him, crunching determinedly through the grain to the ladder, but Timms followed close behind.

'I have my camera in the patrol car. I'll need to take some photographs before I bag the shoe and collect some of that grain.'

Prairie ascended the ladder with the alacrity of an Olympic gymnast. With the air of the open fields on her face, she felt revived and stood with her hands on her hips, breathing deeply. She closed her eyes momentarily but no sooner snapped them open again. The nauseating stain was imprinted on the back of her eyelids, like a horrible negative. Timms came back from the car, the box-like camera with the huge flash slung over his shoulder. Evidence bags sprouted from his pockets like summer lettuces.

Prairie stayed outside as Timms climbed back down into the bowels of the grain pit. She wandered over to the grate and, being careful not to stand on it, peered down. She could see and hear the pops and whirrs of the camera at work.

'Don't stand on the grate, Miss Humble,' Timms called up to her. Prairie rolled her eyes and sang back, 'I won't.' But she scoured the grate for evidence of that same dark stain that spread below. There was nothing visible. The rain had probably washed it away, the only evidence of Briar Lee's life force captured by the thin layer of grain below.

She could see Briar standing by that grate, in her pink ballet slippers, her red satin lips pouting, her platinum hair wild about her shoulders. She saw the taillights of Gil's car, receding in the direction of Wheatsheaf and the warmth of the Harvest Hotel. Was Briar scared at being left out there alone? Or just furious that Gil had called her bluff? Prairie suspected the latter.

And then she saw an assailant. An assailant who had hidden in the entry to the grain pit and had dropped the skeleton key on the threshold. An assailant who had overpowered the tiny tele-phonist on the grate above the grain pit, the struggle causing Briar to lose her shoe. She saw the snowy white flesh of Briar's throat as her platinum hair was yanked backwards with a brutal force, and the flash of a blade as it sliced her carotid artery. And Prairie saw Briar fall like a calf in a slaughterhouse, her blood cascading down through the grate onto the grain.

Had the killer then dumped the lifeless body of Briar Lee in the middle of the highway to be obliterated like roadkill? As Timm's camera flash popped and whined below, Prairie turned away and was sick, as quietly as possible in the shadows of the silo.

○   ○   ○

On Saturday morning, Heck and Maureen Johnson were waiting on the porch when Ted Thurgood's utility vehicle bounced down the long gravel road towards the house. Maureen had spotted the dust flying as soon as the veterinarian turned off the highway, and she called Heck in from the kitchen garden. Ted had barely turned off the ignition when Heck barrelled over.

'Well?' he asked. 'Was it poison?'

'C'mon now, Heck,' said Ted, peeling himself out of the driver's seat. 'I've just driven all the way up from Silky Hills. I'm spitting feathers here. What do you say to a cuppa, Maureen?'

Ted sat at the kitchen table of sturdy oak, hand-carved by Heck's father, and ran his fingers absently over the whorls and nicks from a lifetime of use. Maureen placed a steaming mug of milky coffee in front of him and offered him a slice of cake.

'Don't mind if I do, Maureen,' said Ted. 'I'd drive from Golga every day of the week for a slice of your Victoria sponge.'

'Go on with you,' Maureen countered, blushing.

Heck sat, like a hawk in a tree, watching Ted chew the cake and sip the coffee. When he judged the vet sufficiently recovered from his journey, he said 'Well?'

Ted sighed. 'The tests in the lab confirmed that water to be almost fifteen percent salt, Heck. And that sample came straight from the standpipe, not the trough. That means the underground bore is salt water. My autopsy showed your sheep died of hypernatremia, Heck – abnormally high sodium levels in the blood. Initials symptoms would have been thirst – and the more the sheep drank, the sicker it would have become. Eventually the brain swelled enough to cause death. Did your other sheep show any signs of sickness before they died? Jitteriness, confusion, lethargy?'

'Nope.'

'You said they got all worrisome that other week,' Maureen interjected. 'Just afore that storm we had.'

'That was cos of the storm,' said Heck, irritated. 'Sheep always get worrisome just afore a storm.'

This was news to the veterinarian, but he didn't bother arguing. 'Mind if I take some more samples? I want to bore down into the water-table in that back paddock of yours and collect water from your other standpipes. I reckon the groundwater here has a salinity problem but I'm not sure whether it's confined to that bottom paddock or not.'

'Those salt bastards!' thundered Heck, bringing his huge fist down on the oak table, making the crockery jump.

'Now then, Heck,' said Ted firmly. 'We need to set one thing straight. If that groundwater is salty, that's nothing to do with Blush Saltworks. Christ, man – your farm is on the edge of a salt pan. That low paddock may as well be *in* the lake.' He softened his tone. 'Now, I'm going to call in on Constable Timms when I'm done here, let him know my findings about the sheep and my suspicions about the groundwater. So, you'd better not charge about the town blaming others, you hear? Because soon the truth'll come to light, and you'll look like a right eejit.'

O   O   O

Prairie stayed in bed long past Saturday's breakfast hour at the Harvest Hotel. She couldn't face the wittering of Felice. Constable Timms had sworn her to secrecy about their recent excursion and as such, she didn't wish to talk to anybody but him. It was too awful a burden to bear alone. Every time she closed her eyes that night, visions swarmed of Briar Lee dying alone in the dark.

Felice had left a breakfast tray outside her door – a hot pot of coffee, a little jug of milk, a glass of processed orange juice and a bowl of muesli. A slim, white envelope was tucked between the milk and the coffee pot. Prairie drank the juice, picked at the muesli and made a cup of coffee that ultimately went cold.

As she prised open the envelope, she thought about Gil. She desperately wanted to see him, but Constable Timms had warned that it was not a good idea, especially as he remained the prime suspect in the telephonist's murder and she herself was now implicated in the investigation. Prairie sighed and pulled a folded note out of the envelope. Felice's curlicue handwriting pirouetted across the page.

> *Good morning, my love! Father Childers called for you this morning.*
>
> *He wondered if you could pop in and see Agnes Comfrey sometime soon.*

He thinks she could do with some cheering up.

Fxx

Prairie sighed again. That was the last thing she felt like doing today. No sooner had she thought the thought, a pang of guilt ripped through her. *It's probably the best thing I could do today,* she reasoned.

As she bathed and dressed, another thought occurred to her. She and Constable Timms were working on the assumption that the skeleton key had belonged to Briar Lee's assailant; that the murderer had hid in the utility room leading to the granary pit and had dropped the key, either entering or leaving it.

But what if the key had belonged to the victim? Briar, they now knew – without a shadow of a doubt – was not above eavesdropping and extortion. What then, if she was also not above unauthorised entry when the mood took her? What if blackmail had not earned enough for her luxuries? Would she have been tempted to turn to burglary and petty theft?

On the other hand, thought Prairie with a sharp prick of conscience, there was also nothing to suggest that Briar Lee had stooped to breaking and entering. It was an interesting perspective, one that she would be sure to talk over with the constable when she got to the police station.

○   ○   ○

'A ham and salad roll, please Rosie, love, but no beetroot. And one of those little cakes – one with the pink icing, I think. I'm in a pink mood.'

'Right you are, Olive,' said Rosie-Mandy cheerfully. 'Any news on the lines?'

'They are close,' said Olive. 'One of the technicians rowed across the creek last night to let me know they'll commence testing the lines later today.'

'Oh! That's great news! It must be so boring sitting at a switchboard with nothing to do.' Rosie-Mandy shoved a small pink cupcake into a bag and twisted it carefully so as not to smudge the icing.

'Let's just say I'm down to my last Mills & Boon and the library bus isn't here for another week.' They laughed. The bell rang behind her and Olive turned.

'Prairie! Good news! The lines should be up by this afternoon.'

'About time,' said Prairie. She sounded more churlish than she'd meant to.

Olive frowned. 'Are you alright. You look terribly dark underneath the eyes, my dear. Late night?'

'Not overly,' Prairie lied. 'I guess I mustn't have slept as well as I thought I did. Rosie, may I have one of those teacakes, please? And perhaps a slice of Battenberg.' She turned to Olive. 'I'm on my way to see Agnes Comfrey. Father Childers has asked me to call in on her. It must be ever such a lonesome burden for her, having to make all those arrangements on her own. I'm sure I couldn't do it.'

Olive nodded sympathetically. 'Shall I call you there once I know the lines are back?'

'Oh yes! Please do. If I haven't heard from you by the time I'm ready to leave, I'll call past the exchange and wait with you.'

Anything to take my mind off Gil and that silo, she thought.

O   O   O

As she drove down Grain Street towards the Comfrey residence, Prairie saw the patrol car in the station driveway. She parked out the front and making sure Jonetta Williams and Sylvia Hamer were nowhere in sight, she ducked in.

'Prairie!' said Constable Timms, delighted to see her. 'Are you alright? That was a frightful discovery yesterday. I've been worried about you.'

She handed him a paper bag. 'I'm quite alright,' she assured him, lying once more. 'A slice of Battenberg for your morning tea,' she said.

Timms patted his hands together excitedly. It was rare that anyone in the town showed him this kind of friendship. *I hope Miss Humble doesn't turn out to be the murderer,* he thought fleetingly. *That would be a terrible shame.* 'Good news,' he said. 'You may as well be the first to know, although I suppose that honour really should go to Mr Sanders…'

Prairie's heart dropped a beat. 'What is it?'

'Ted Thurgood – the vet – called in here this morning on his way back to Blackwatch. He'd been out to see Heck Johnson. Seems the cause of the sheep's death was salty groundwater from the standpipe in that lower paddock.'

Prairie bit her lip. 'Gil said it would be that.'

Timms nodded. 'He did indeed. Ted's doing some more testing on Heck's property. See how widespread the issue is. It may just be that bottom paddock…'

'For now,' said Prairie, glumly.

'For now,' agreed Timms. 'But at least we can put a stop to rumours that Mr Sanders was responsible for the sheep's death.'

'Yes,' said Prairie. 'I hope we are soon able to put a stop to rumours that he might be responsible for Briar's. I wanted to run something past you,' she said.

'Shall I make tea?'

'No, not for me thanks, I'm on my way – oh! I ran into Olive in the *Caff.* She tells me the technicians are very close to repair and hopefully we'll be reconnected by this afternoon. Isn't that wonderful news?'

'Yes,' said Timms. 'That is good news indeed. It's certainly taken them long enough. Now if we can only get that problematic bridge repaired. What did you want to talk about?'

Prairie wondered aloud if the key had belonged to Briar Lee all along. 'If Barry Skipton says the key isn't one of his, then perhaps it's come from elsewhere, like Golga. Tell me, Constable,' – she still wasn't comfortable with calling him *'Emmanuel'* – 'have there been any reports of petty theft in the area over the past few months? Burglaries, break-ins – anything like that – that you haven't been able to solve?'

'Farming implements occasionally disappear from barns and the like,' said Timms. 'But nothing in the town springs to mind.'

'Well,' said Prairie. 'It was just a thought. It might help to explain how she was able to afford all that jewellery and clothing.'

'This is true,' said Timms, his mind preoccupied with the Battenberg cake. 'I shall give it some thought.'

○　○　○

Baby Blue nosed into the Comfrey's driveway beneath its arch of trees and stopped behind the yellow Ford Escort. Prairie looked at the teacake on the seat beside her. *I hope you don't end up in the bin,* she thought.

She skipped up the steps and rang the bell. Agnes did not answer. She rang again and waited a few minutes, but when Agnes still did not come to the door, Prairie followed the veranda around to the back of the house. From the shed came the sound of things falling – or being thrown – and Prairie worried the shed was being ransacked.

'Agnes,' she called, uncertainly. 'It's Prairie.'

The shed fell silent.

'Agnes?' Prairie called again.

Agnes Comfrey stepped from the shed and Prairie almost gasped aloud. She was red-faced and wild-eyed. Her hair was dishevelled, and she looked as though she had not slept.

'Prairie!' she said and tried to smooth her grubby apron.

'I, I didn't mean to disturb you,' Prairie murmured. It was on the tip of her tongue to mention she'd called in at the request of Father Childers, but something about Agnes' countenance stopped her. 'I brought us a teacake. I thought we might have morning tea together?'

Agnes' face softened. 'Where are my manners?' she said, rushing forward. 'Prairie! How thoughtful! Oh dear, I look a mess. I've been clearing out the shed.'

'I heard,' said Prairie, following Agnes indoors. 'I worried for a minute that you were being burgled.' *How could I think Briar was a petty thief?* she chided herself.

Agnes laughed as she filled the cast iron kettle and set it on the range. 'I was looking for something,' she said. 'I can't find it anywhere, and I am afraid I've been turning things upside down.' She smiled but Prairie noticed she looked very, very tired. 'Will you give me a moment to fix myself up while the kettle boils?'

'Of course,' said Prairie. 'How about I slice the cake?'

'Yes, marvellous,' called Agnes, rushing out of the room. Prairie opened the dresser draw and took out a bone-handled bread knife.

'Shall we use the forget-me-not plates?' she called.

'Yes! Yes, please! In the dresser,' Agnes' voice came from the bathroom over the sound of a running tap.

Prairie busied herself setting the kitchen table for tea, neatly arranging the sliced cake on plates and filling the pot with tea leaves from a blue and white striped Cornishware tea caddy. The blackened cast-iron frying pan sat on the range next to the kettle and Prairie was careful not to knock the handle as she bustled about.

Agnes reappeared looking refreshed. She had brushed her hair and swept it up into a bun. She'd washed her face and put on a clean, lemon tabard over her drab, grey housedress. She took over the tea-making and bid Prairie sit down.

'I sit down all day at work,' laughed Prairie. 'It's nice to have something to do. I miss a kitchen. Although, I am reluctant to mention that to Felice, as she might put me to work during the breakfast and dinner rush!' Agnes laughed with her and filled the teapot with scalding water. She seemed in brighter spirits now.

'What did you lose?' asked Prairie, settling down at the table.

'Pardon?' Agnes swirled the teapot to help the leaves steep.

'You said you were looking for something. Oh, thank you,' Prairie gratefully accepted a slice of cake. She was hungry now, having picked at her breakfast.

Agnes poured the tea and sighed. 'A necklace,' she said. 'It was terribly sentimental. My father gave it to me.'

'Oh no! Can you remember when you had it last?'

'I wear it all the time. It's never off. I fear the chain has broken somewhere and it's slipped off without me knowing.' Her eyes filled with tears, and she blinked furiously to hold them back.

'What did it look like?' asked Prairie.

'It was just a silver chain. Nothing fancy, but it was sentimental.'

Prairie thought about her conversation with Constable Timms but quickly dismissed the idea that Agnes' necklace might have been stolen. As she said, it was always around her neck.

'Thick or thin?' asked Prairie.

'Pardon?'

'Your necklace. Was the chain thick or thin? I'll be sure to keep an eye out for it. It may have come off down the street. I'm happy to call into the shops along Grain Street and ask if anybody has handed it in, if you like?'

'Oh,' said Agnes. 'Yes, that would be lovely. Just if you go in. Don't make a special trip. I'm sure it will turn up. Not particularly thick, in answer to your question, but definitely not thin.'

'Well, that narrows it down,' said Prairie, good-naturedly. 'Oh, good news about the telephone lines! Olive says they are close to repair. Hopefully, we'll be reconnected very soon.'

'Wonderful,' said Agnes, sipping her tea. 'Not that it matters much to me, I suppose. Nobody ever calls me, and I have nobody to call. But you must be excited to be going back to work?'

'Yes,' said Prairie, biting into the soft cake. 'I suppose I am. This is delicious.' She chewed and swallowed. 'In fact, Olive said she would call me here once the lines are back up. I hope that's alright. I'll have to go back to the exchange when that happens – there's only three of us to cover the day shifts now and I suspect the whole town will be wanting to talk to someone as soon as we are reconnected.'

Agnes nodded in agreement, but Prairie suddenly felt awkward. Everyone would be wanting to talk to someone – except Agnes. She changed the subject. 'Any news yet on when you might have the funeral,' she asked gently, but Agnes shook her head.

'I hope it's soon. It's hard to move forward.'

Prairie patted her hand sympathetically. 'If there is anything I can do to help…' Agnes placed her hand on top of Prairie's.

'You are very kind indeed, Prairie Humble. You may just be,' she said, shyly, looking down, 'my only friend.'

O O O

Olive Wellshorn reclined in the switch operator's chair as far as it would go and her stockinged feet, free of shoes, were up on the desk, the door firmly snipped behind her. *His firm tongue was circling the areola of her left breast.* Olive tingled. The rude buzz of the switchboard lighting up was an unexpected shock.

'Jesus Christ!' cried Olive and the paperback novel flew over her shoulder. She leaned forward, her heart pounding and stared disbelievingly at the switchboard, flashing furiously away, begging to be answered. She grabbed her headset and stuffed the jack into its slot. 'Wheatsheaf, 5546,' she breathed.

'Hey Olive, tech check at Brewer's Hill. Line coming through okay?'

'Line coming in loud and clear, Sid.' Olive rolled her eyes. Why now?

'I think we're back up and running, old girl!' The chirpiness in the technician's voice irritated her.

'Thanks Sid,' she said. 'But enough of the *'Old Girl,'* hey?'

Olive disconnected and quickly plugged through to the Comfrey residence. The people of Wheatsheaf had been checking their phones obsessively since the storm. It was only a matter of time before the first resident picked up the phone and heard the familiar hum of the dial tone. She was, in the words of Briar Lee, *'about to get smashed.'* Olive smiled ruefully, thinking about the girl, and dialled Agnes Comfrey. The line clicked and clicked again. There was no answer. The switchboard lit up. Olive moved the jack.

'Wheatsheaf. Number please?'

'Olive? Are we back? It's Prunella Battersby. Thank God and His Heavenly Host of Warrior Angels. Can you get me Irma Vickery? It's an emergency.'

Zip stuck again? thought Olive, rolling her eyes. 'Connecting,' she said, brightly. The switch lit up again. *Shit!* Olive moved the jack once more.

'This is the coroner's office in Golga. Get me Constable Timms please. I've been trying for three days.'

She plugged in the jack, dialled the station and connected the call. When Timms answered, she said, 'It's the coroner.' Connecting the call, she said 'Go ahead please.' The switch lit up elsewhere, but Olive ignored the blinking lights. Slowly, she pushed the switch key forward and held her breath.

'Timms? This is Ivan Jacowiesz, coroner in Golga.'

'Sir, good to hear from you.'

'I've been trying this damned phone number for three days!'

'Yes, Sir. We had a storm on Wednesday. Unfortunately, it took out the telephone lines at Brewer's Hill – and the bridge over the Golga River. I need to report a…'

'Never mind that,' said Jacowiesz. 'I've conducted the autopsy on that Comfrey woman.'

Timms leaned forward in his chair. With all the recent activity around Briar Lee, he'd mostly forgotten about Gwinny Comfrey. He reached for his notepad.

'Sir?'

'Gwinevere Comfrey's death was *not* the result of a fall. She died from direct blunt force trauma to the left side of the skull. Temporal bone is shattered. A shard pierced the temporal lobe leading to intercranial haemorrhage.' Timms was silent. 'Are you there?'

'Sir?' said Timms, not fully comprehending. 'Are you suggesting someone struck Gwinny Comfrey…deliberately?'

'Well, she didn't bloody do it to herself, Timms!' Jacowiesz thundered.

21

Silver and Iron

'Snap!' Agnes Comfrey's hand slammed down on the kitchen table. She raked the cards inwards.

'I'm afraid you are far too good at this for me, Agnes dear,' said Prairie. She looked at her watch. It was a quarter to one in the afternoon. She had spent almost two hours in the company of Agnes Comfrey.

'Do you mind if I use your phone, Agnes. I want to see if the lines are up yet?'

Agnes collected the cards and smoothed them, ready for their box. 'Of course,' she said.

Prairie thought she detected a hint of disappointment. 'I just don't want to leave Olive at the exchange all by herself if the lines come back up.'

Agnes nodded. Prairie pushed back her chair and wandered into the living room. She picked up the heavy Bakelite receiver, but it was silent. She tapped the cradle but there was no response. Replacing the cradle, Prairie bumped a slim wooden vase that sat beside it on the telephone table. It was as light as a feather and toppled sideways. Prairie lunged for it, but it fell, spilling its contents onto the carpet. Prairie cursed under her breath and dropped to her hands and knees. With amazement, she held up a broken silver rope chain. Not particularly thick, but definitely not thin.

○ ○ ○

Olive cursed when the coroner hung up. Before she could let Emmanuel Timms know she was still on the line, the constable disconnected the call. She dialled back immediately, but there was no answer. Was he trying to call her? She watched the switchboard, but it was silent. With trembling fingers, she inserted the jack and dialled the Comfrey residence. No answer there either.

'*Fuck!*' screamed Olive. '*Somebody answer the goddamn phone!*'

○ ○ ○

Sitting back on her haunches, Prairie held up the broken silver chain in wonder. She was about to call out to Agnes when she noticed the telephone cord was not plugged in. She leaned in beneath the telephone table and connected the device. She picked up the receiver and heard the comforting hum of the dial tone. Overjoyed, she replaced the cradle and with one hand clutching the silver chain, she pulled herself up using the armchair for support. She was about to cry out for Agnes again when the telephone rang shrilly, giving her a start.

'*Oh!*' She stared at it for a moment, laughed and then answered.

'Hello?'

'Prairie? Is that you?'

'Olive, dear! Why yes! How marvellous the lines are back! Is it dreadfully busy?

'Prairie, listen to me. Is Agnes there? Just answer '*yes*' or '*no.*''

'Wha..?'

'Yes or no?' Olive's tone concerned her.

'Yes.'

'Listen to me, but pretend we are discussing work. I've just put the coroner through to Constable Timms. The coroner believes Gwinny Comfrey was murdered!'

'What?' Prairie almost dropped the receiver.

'Be light. Pretend we are discussing work.'

Prairie could hardly force her lips to move, never mind command her voice to speak.

'Uh huh,' she said dumbly.

'You have to get out of there, Prairie. I tried to call Timms to let him know you're there, but I can't reach him.'

'How?' was all Prairie could muster. 'How?' she said again, hoping Olive would get her meaning.

'Smashed in the head with something. Prairie, please just get off the phone and come straight here.'

'I will,' said Prairie and let the heavy receiver fall into the cradle.

'I see our lines are repaired.'

Prairie whirled about. She had not heard Agnes approach. Agnes was smiling but when her gaze landed on the necklace in Prairie's hand a look of confusion swept over her. Prairie followed her gaze and held out the chain.

'I'm sorry. I knocked the vase over and this fell out. Could this be the necklace you are looking for?'

Agnes's eyes glittered. 'Why yes! Yes, thank you. How clever of you to have found it for me.'

'That is the necklace you were looking for?'

'Yes. Yes, it is. Thank you, Prairie.'

'It's broken. But it was in the vase.'

'Why, so it was. I remember now. It broke a while ago and I put it in the vase. I had forgotten all about it. Well, never mind. I have it back now. Was that Olive? You'll be wanted back at the exchange now. I'm sure all of Wheatsheaf wants to speak with somebody.' Agnes' face was grim. She took Prairie by the arm and tried to lead her toward the front door. Prairie gently placed a hand on Agnes' wrist to loosen the grip.

'I have to get my purse,' she said and turned back to the kitchen. She calmly collected her handbag from where it hung on the back of a kitchen chair and that's when she saw it.

The time-worn, blackened, cast iron frying pan, sitting on the range.

She saw herself and Olive with Briar Lee on Tuesday night in the crowded Harvest Hotel. She was drinking Guinness; Briar had a glass of Chablis. Briar's platinum locks danced about her shoulders as she tossed her head and said…what was it that she had said?

I saw that Dag-nes Comfrey in Carlson's, too.

What was she doing in there?

Dunno. Buying a new frying pan, I guess.

Prairie hugged her purse to her chest and as lightly as possible said 'I've always wanted a sturdy frying pan. Do you think I could get something like that in Carlson's?'

Agnes snorted. 'Carlson's? Hardly. They don't make them like that, anymore. That was my…' She stopped and the word caught in her throat.

'Was it your mother's?' Prairie asked quietly, cautiously. Agnes looked at the frying pan with the same wild-eyed stare Prairie had seen when she emerged from the shed. Her eyes were so dark they glittered like feldspar.

'Mother's, yes. Everything was Mother's,' said Agnes, quietly. 'The house was Mother's, the money was Mother's, my father was Mother's, I was Mother's. Nothing here that wasn't *hers.*' She spat the last word.

'What were you looking for in the shed, Agnes?'

Agnes tore her eyes from the frying pan and stared straight at Prairie. Her eyes were soft and brown again. 'I told you, Prairie, dear. My necklace. My father gave it to me.' Agnes held the silver chain to her right cheek and closed her eyes. 'You brought it back to me. Thank you, Prairie. You are a true friend. I don't know what I'd do without you.'

'What was on the necklace, Agnes?' asked Prairie gently, still clutching her purse to her chest.

'What do you mean?' Agnes' eyes snapped open, hard and dark once more.

'Was there a charm on your necklace, perhaps?' asked Prairie, trying to sound nonchalant but failing. Agnes watched her with the piercing gaze of a falcon.

'What...do you mean?' Agnes asked again, slowly and deliberately this time.

'I don't think you were looking for your necklace, Agnes,' Prairie said, so quietly she was almost whispering. 'I think you were looking for something that was *on* the necklace.'

Agnes stared at Prairie with such a cold gaze that Prairie felt her knees buckle. But for the grip of those eyes, she would have collapsed.

'Such as?' Agnes counted, whispering back.

'A key?'

The black Bakelite phone shrilled, demanding attention. Prairie jumped. Agnes ignored it, her gaze firmly fixed on Prairie. Prairie dared not – could not – look away. 'We should answer that,' she murmured.

'No,' snapped Agnes. 'No one wants to talk to the Comfreys. Must be a wrong number,' she hissed. The phone trilled until it rang out. The silence left in its wake was crushing. Prairie struggled to breathe.

'No one wants to talk to the Comfreys,' Agnes said again, working the silver chain through her fingers like a set of worry-beads, 'Except you, Prairie Humble. The whole town despises us. Stupid...Bigoted...' she seemed to want to utter something else but refrained. 'At least they mostly left us alone. But not you, Prairie Humble. Everything is...*pleasant* in your world.' She spat the word. 'Can't leave the fringe-dwellers to dwell on the fringe in your world – no!' She scoffed but quickly softened.

'No one has ever shown us any kindness, except for Father Childers. But you, you brought us a sponge-cake. Not dog shit through the letter box. Or rocks through the window. That's what we used to get, from our beloved townsfolk. If they were not hurling eggs at our front door, they were hurling insults when we passed them in the street. Did you know that passionfruit was my favourite flavour?' She smiled and there were tears in her eyes. 'You brought me a passionfruit sponge and it was the most beautiful thing.'

'So why did it end up in the bin?' Prairie asked. Agnes looked as though she'd been slapped. The tears welling in her eyes spilled down her cheeks.

'It went in the bin,' she whispered, 'because Agnes Comfrey doesn't deserve the kindness of strangers.' She looked at Prairie, a trembling, wounded bird.

'I don't understand,' said Prairie. 'Help me to understand, Agnes.'

The telephone rent the air again. 'Shut *up!*' Agnes roared and hurled the Cornishware tea-caddy at the wall. It shattered and Prairie cowered. When the phone rang off, some of Agnes' passion simmered with it. She seemed calmer.

'My mother was a hateful woman, Prairie Humble. Nasty. I don't wonder the town hated her. But they didn't need to hate me. I was never unkind to a living soul. Not once. But people hate what they fear, don't they? Mother was jealous that you should have looked at *me*, and pitied *me*, and brought *me* a cake. My favourite flavour. *'Look, Mother,'* I said on the day of your visit. *'Prairie Humble has brought us a cake. Passionfruit sponge. That's my favourite.'* I set it on the table, so perfect and sunny with its yellow icing. I fetched the forget-me-not China and turned to fill the kettle for our tea. And my mother took her fist and slammed it into the cake as though she were a judge, over and over and over. And then she just looked at me and said *'Oops.''*

'Oh Agnes,' said Prairie, her heart aching and pounding in equal measure. 'I…I'm so sorry. I never meant to cause such a problem for you. If I'd known…I never would have…'

A brittle, hollow rattle that in other circumstances might have been a laugh came from Agnes Comfrey. *'I* knew, Prairie. *I* knew, at that moment, I could no longer ignore it.' Agnes looked across at the range and took a step towards it.

'I spent so many years dependent on that woman. I thought I didn't know how to live without her. But you brought a passionfruit sponge to the house. And I realised in that moment, for fifty years, I had just existed. I wanted to *live.* Just a bit. Just for a while.' She picked up the heavy frying pan and looked at it.

'I barely remember the impact. All I know is that when I saw what she had done to my cake, my beautiful cake – and that she was *laughing* – well I just wanted to obliterate her spiteful, sneering face. I don't even think I thought. I just acted. There it was, where it always is, on the range. Trusted and heavy. I picked it up and I swung. I think it must have been satisfying. I remember that, feeling *victorious* afterwards, although I don't remember the impact. She went flying across the room. I could almost laugh when I think of it, although I mustn't, for that is truly wicked, and that is not what I am. I'm a good girl, Prairie Humble. My father always said so. My mother never liked that. And then I thought, what to do? So, I dragged her into the living room – she was so very light – and I pulled the bookshelf down on her. That was heavier, of course.'

Prairie was stunned. She swallowed hard. 'And Briar?' she whispered.

'What of her?' snapped Agnes, suddenly cold again.

'Did you kill Briar, Agnes?'

'Who cares?'

'*I* care,' said Prairie, quietly. 'She was my friend.'

Agnes snorted. 'That little slut was nobody's friend,' she spat. 'Don't kid yourself, Prairie Humble! She was a cold, vain, uncaring little bitch who was only out for herself.'

'Why did she die, Agnes?' said Prairie, her voice stronger now. 'Tell me.'

Agnes paced the room, gnashing her teeth, working her jaw left and right, hugging the frying pan to her chest. 'She saw,' she said eventually. 'I didn't know that, but she saw. Car broke down. She was at the kitchen window, but I didn't see. I didn't know. Cornered me in Carlson's on Tuesday. Thrust a new frying pan at me. Told me I should buy a new one. Didn't I need a new one? I asked her what she was on about. Then she tried to blackmail me.'

Prairie held her breath. 'What happened the night Briar died, Agnes?'

Agnes shrugged.

'Did you follow Briar to the silo?'

'I did *not!*' Agnes snapped. 'I was *already at* the silo.'

'What were you doing there?'

'I *always* go there,' Agnes said, defensively. 'It's *my* place,' she paced back and forth. 'I do my best thinking there. I feel close to my father there. I ask him questions and he gives me the answers.'

Prairie thought back to their day at Blush Lake. 'The skeleton key that opens the locks to the grain pit and the shed – that belonged to you?'

Agnes rocked backwards and forwards, hugging the frying pan and working the silver chain through her fingers. 'Was my father's,' she mumbled.

'That was on the silver chain?'

Agnes nodded dumbly.

'That day I picked you up, you said you had come back from the Church, but Father Childers hadn't seen you that day, had he? You were out at the silos, weren't you? To look for the key? You thought you might have dropped it there?'

Agnes just shrugged.

'Oh Agnes,' said Prairie. 'What happened that night?'

Agnes was quiet for a long time. Prairie was sure she could hear her heart beating.

'I was in the grain pit because that's where I go,' the woman said eventually, sighing. She let the frying pan drop to her side. 'I go there to think. I wanted to think about what to do about my mother, and about that hateful little strumpet extorting me. Then I heard them. First the cars. Then they were arguing above the grate. She was trying to blackmail him too!'

'Gil?'

Agnes nodded. 'Such a little bitch. She was angry because he wouldn't pay up. He kept saying that she had it all wrong. She threatened to go to Constable Timms, and he told her *'Go right ahead.'* Then he left. She went berserk, screaming and stomping her feet. Such a brat. She caught her foot on the grate, and one of her shoes fell off. Damn near hit me in the face. She bent down to look through the grate with her torch and that's when she saw me. Starts to laugh. Accuses me of being a crazy eavesdropper! *Me,* while she's going around looking in windows and blackmailing half the town! Says she's going to come and lock me in, all ready for Constable Timms to arrest me. I couldn't let that happen. I flew up the ladder and collided with her, just as she was coming into the access room. We struggled. I guess that's when my necklace broke – the chain slid into my bra, but I didn't notice that until I got home. She punched me and ran. I chased her and caught up with her by the grate and…'

'You slit her throat?'

Agnes looked down and nodded.

'You carry a knife?' Prairie asked, incredulous.

'Always,' said Agnes flatly. 'You would too, if you grew up the way I did, if the town despised you the way they despised me. People are capable of the most despicable things.' This time, Agnes did not drop her gaze. She stared straight at Prairie, her eyes hard obsidian.

Prairie tried not to flinch under that gaze. For Briar, and for Gil. 'What then?' she asked, her jaw set. Inside, her blood was a torrent.

'I just left her. I ran home, though the fields. I didn't know what to do.'

'You didn't drag her into the road?'

'*No!*' said Agnes and she seemed genuinely aghast. 'No! I thought she was dead when I left, but perhaps she wasn't. Maybe she crawled…I don't know. I…I supposed that eventually she would be found, and your friend would be blamed. I'm… I am honestly very sorry for that.'

The phone rang again, splitting the silence.

'I'm going to get that,' said Prairie firmly. 'They know I'm here. They'll just keep ringing if I don't answer it.'

'No,' said Agnes, taking a menacing step forward.

'Agnes, please. It's no use. Constable Timms knows about your mother, and he knows I'm here. Just let me get the phone.'

'No,' said Agnes, firmer now. There was no softness in her eyes. 'He doesn't know about Briar Lee,' she said. 'Nor will he.' Agnes swung the frying pan once again. Prairie heard the sickening thud as it made contact with the side of her head. And then nothing.

22

It's All Over Now, Baby Blue

The smell was familiar. A dankness with a woody overlay. Musky, the tell-tale sign of mice. Prairie almost gagged. Her head throbbed. Her shoulder ached too. She opened her eyes into blackness. Had she lost her vision? Slowly, shapes came into focus, aided by the soft shafts of light filtering down from above.

Prairie guessed at once where she was. She was sitting upright against a wall, her legs stretched out in front of her. Her shoulders and wrists burned, and she quickly understood why. Her hands were bound behind her back with a cord. It bit cruelly. She guessed it was the same type of cord that bound her ankles together.

'Agnes?' she called into the gloom, but her throat was parched, and she only managed a croak. She swallowed and tried again. *'Help! Please!'* Prairie whimpered and thought of Gil. The tears began to flow. Sweet Gil, completely innocent of any wrongdoing, to sheep or telephonist, but hated by the town anyway. She closed her eyes and leaned her head back against the wall, sobbing and trying to communicate with him by telepathy.

Please Gil, I'm here. I'm so scared. Please help me.

She thought of Constable Timms and Olive and sent silent pleas to them as well.

Olive! She took a deep breath and opened her eyes, swallowing her tears. Olive knew she was at the Comfrey place when the news of Gwinny's death reached Constable Timms! *Surely* Olive had relayed that news to Timms by now. The repeated ringing of Agnes Comfrey's Bakelite phone had to be one of them, or the other – or perhaps both?

Surely?

Prairie clung to the word – *surely* after receiving word from the coroner that Gwinny Comfrey had been bludgeoned to death, Timms would be on his way to arrest Agnes? And when he failed to locate her at the house, surely, he'd look….

Where? Where would he look? Prairie slumped against the wall. There was no reason for Timms to look for her here in the grain pit at the Golden Grain silo. This place was connected to the death of Briar Lee – not Gwinny Comfrey – and Emmanuel Timms had no idea about Agnes Comfrey's connection to the silo. She alone knew that.

Emmanuel Timms. *Emmanuel. I'll never get to call him that now.* Prairie's eyes welled with tears. How ridiculous and unthinkable some things seemed on stable ground. Yet, when the earth threatened to plummet beneath you, what you would not give for the ridiculous and unthinkable.

Well observed, Prairie, my girl. That was her father's voice. The tears welled momentarily and stopped. Prairie sniffed.

You are not some princess in a tower, she chided herself roughly. *Nobody is coming to your rescue. You, my dear, are going to have to rescue yourself.* Her tears gave way to anger. Pure, controlled, useful anger. And despite the raw agony of it, she clenched her teeth and began to twist her wrists this way and that.

○ ○ ○

In the exchange, Olive was ready to abandon her post. She'd called Timms, then the Comfreys and when she got no answer at either, she called Timms again. She almost cried with relief when he finally picked up.

'Wheatsheaf Police.'

'Emmanuel, it's Olive…'

'I can't talk just now, Miss Wellshorn. I am preparing myself for…an arrest.'

'Now,' said Olive. 'You have to go now.'

'Pardon?'

'Prairie is with Agnes Comfrey. I'm worried. I called the Comfrey's place and spoke to Prairie. I told her about the call from the coroner and warned her to get out of there as soon as possible…'

'You did *what?*' Timms squawked. 'How did you know about…? You telephonists are incorrigible! I'll be having a word with Fidel Peterson when this is all over.'

'Please!' Olive shouted, exasperated. 'I told Prairie to come straight to the exchange, but she hasn't! That was almost two hours ago. And I've called the Comfreys another five times since then, but nobody picks up! Please, Emmanuel! I'm frightened. I'm worried that something has happened to Prairie. What if Agnes overheard our conversation and knows that Prairie is aware of what she did to her own mother?'

Timms sat in a stunned silence, ticking over the awful possibilities.

'Are you there?'

'Yes, Olive. I'm here,' Timms said quietly. 'I'll head out to the Comfrey place straight away.'

'If you find Prairie, will you bring her to the exchange? Please? I want to know she's alright.'

'Yes. Yes, of course.'

'And if you don't find her, will you please come straight to the exchange and tell me? I'll help you look.'

'Yes. Yes. Fine. I must go, Miss Wellshorn. Try not to worry,' he said, hanging up, worrying enough for them both.

Prairie strained against her bonds until she was sure she'd slice right through her wrists. The pain, excruciating at first, petered into numbness. Prairie doubted this was a good sign. She started when a door opened somewhere above to her left. Footsteps rang out on metal. Somebody was climbing down the ladder. She held little hope that the person was anyone other than Agnes Comfrey. Footsteps crunched across the grain towards her. Prairie stared up at her captor.

Agnes had changed into a pair of denim overalls and a chequered shirt. Heavy leather work boots hugged her feet. In her hand she carried a torch and a water bottle on a toggle rope. She knelt beside Prairie and unscrewed the cap of the bottle.

'I'm so sorry I had to do that to you, Prairie,' she said and to her surprise, Prairie thought she sounded remorseful. 'Here, I've brought you some water. I'll help you drink.'

The apology sent a wave of fury through Prairie. 'Have you poisoned the water to finish me off?' As soon as the words were out of her mouth, she regretted them. She was so thirsty. Agnes looked stung.

'Here,' she said. 'I'll drink first. I can assure you I have not poisoned the water.' She gulped swiftly and then offered the bottle to Prairie. Chastened, Prairie nodded. Agnes held the bottle to her lips and helped her drink. The water tasted so good.

'I didn't set out to kill my mother, Prairie. Or Briar Lee. I swear; I'm no murderer.'

'Yet here we are,' Prairie retorted. Her fear and her vulnerability made her angry and she wanted to lash out in every hurtful way possible, like a wounded animal. She knew she had to reign it in. She was completely helpless. Agnes had the upper hand. Agnes sighed and sat down in the chaff.

'How did I get down here?' Prairie asked. 'My head hurts. It's throbbing. Am I bleeding?'

'I'm sorry about that,' said Agnes, taking a handkerchief out of her pocket. 'I did cut you a little bit.' She doused some water on the piece of cloth and gently wiped Prairie's left temple. Prairie winced. She was horrified when Agnes pulled the cloth away, stained darkly with her own blood.

'I tried to get you down the ladder as gently as possible. Luckily you are light as a bird, although I am afraid, I did drop you part way down. I don't think you broke any bones. I tried to check.'

Prairie stared at the woman aghast. *You're deranged,* she thought. 'What now?' she asked. 'Surely you can't mean to leave me here like this?' That word, again. *Surely.*

'I wish you hadn't come to the house,' said Agnes, glumly. Did she mean *today* or *ever*? It was not lost on Prairie that, but for her passionfruit sponge and overwhelming need to be kind, Gwinny Comfrey might still be alive, and by virtue of that, Briar Lee. 'Where did you find my key?'

'It was on the threshold of the door to this place. I came to draw the sunrise. I would probably have missed it, but for the morning sun, shining where it did.'

'Ah,' said Agnes. 'And I suppose the good Constable has it now? I thought so. We were lucky he took the lock away too, or we wouldn't have been able to get in again.'

Damn! thought Prairie. At the time, removing the lock had seemed a good idea. She disliked the way Agnes used the word *'we.'*

'I was mortified to have lost it,' said Agnes. 'It belonged to my father. It opens more locks than you can imagine. But you mustn't think I go around breaking into people's houses, Prairie Humble. I only use it to get in here. I like to come here.'

'What happened to your father?' Prairie asked. It was a calculated question. She wanted to soften Agnes, to keep her talking for as long as possible while she worked on the cord behind her back. She hoped fervently that the Constable and Olive would find her.

A pained look crossed Agnes' face. 'They said he was attempting to clear grain from the wall of the bin next door. It came down like an avalanche and engulfed him. Nobody knew he was in there. He was working by himself. He suffocated to death. A horrible way to go, dying alone.' She looked up, and her dark eyes hardened. 'Nobody knows you're here, Prairie. But you won't die alone, I promise. I shan't be far away.'

An icy wave swept over Prairie. 'Sooner or later,' she said evenly, 'Olive or Constable Timms is bound to go to your house and see my car in the driveway.'

Agnes hugged her knees to her chest and regarded Prairie. 'I'm afraid they won't, Prairie dear,' she said, sadly. 'I thought about that. So, I drove us here in your car.'

Prairie stared at her, aghast, not daring to believe what came next.

'It's in the dam, now,' said Agnes. 'With Briar's Mini. On the other side of the train tracks. I couldn't risk anybody seeing it.'

Prairie's eyes filled with tears. They burned like acid streaking down her face.

'How could you?' she screamed at Agnes. She felt such hatred in that moment that, if her hands were free, she would have lunged at the woman.

O   O   O

The patrol car pulled into the driveway and parked behind the yellow Escort, blocking it in. There was no sign of Baby Blue. Timms exhaled in relief. He hoped Agnes Comfrey would come to the police station quietly. He touched his revolver, though, just to make sure it was there, and checked his cuffs were in the right position.

Mounting the rickety porch steps, he tugged at the clapper of the doorbell. When there was no answer, he rapped loudly and said, 'Agnes, this is Constable Timms. I need you to open the door.' He waited a moment and rapped again. Silence. He peered in through the front window but could see nothing beyond the net curtain.

He walked around the veranda to the back and knocked again. He tried the back door and, mercifully, found it unlocked. He walked through the kitchen and noted the rinsed teacups and plates stacked on the draining board. A deck of playing cards sat on the dining table next to some photographs.

'Agnes?' he called. There was no reply. Timms stalked into the living room and looked about, nonplussed. He picked up the Bakelite telephone and dialled Olive at the exchange. 'Is Miss Humble there with you?' he asked.

'No!' said Olive, her voice high-pitched.

Timms hung up, with instructions that Olive was to call straight back if Prairie arrived at the exchange in the next ten minutes. He wandered back into the kitchen.

And saw it.

He wondered how he had missed it the first time.

There, on a white square of the black and white chequered linoleum floor, was a small but vivid red smear. Timms crouched down and gingerly touched the spot with his index finger. There was no mistaking it. But to whom did it belong?

Timms called the Aid Station and asked whether Miss Humble or Miss Comfrey had attended that day.

They had not.

He called the hospital at Golga and asked for admissions. He searched the house from top to bottom and finding no sign of either Prairie Humble or Agnes Comfrey, he gunned the engine of the patrol car and headed for the exchange.

○ ○ ○

Prairie could no longer see Agnes, but she could hear her moving about in the storeroom above. From the ladder-well, something fell to the floor of the grain pit with a metallic thud. Agnes' heavy tread climbed down after it. There was the sound of Agnes dragging something across the floor, then splashing it about. And then there was the smell of… petrol?

'Agnes, what are you doing?' Prairie called, unable to keep the alarm out of her voice. Agnes didn't answer. 'Agnes?' Prairie almost screamed.

The fumes were unmistakable. Agnes appeared with a jerry-can, dousing the room indiscriminately. When she'd emptied the can, she tossed it aside and stood there gasping for breath.

'I'm sorry, Prairie,' she said. 'I really am. You were a good friend to me. I wish I could have been a better friend to you.'

'Agnes, please!' Prairie could hardly get the words out. 'You don't have to do this!' Sobs racked her chest.

'I'm so sorry, Prairie Humble,' Agnes said again and pulled a book of matches out of her overall breast pocket. She struck one. It flared.

'*Gil!*' Prairie screamed. Then mustering all her strength, as though she had to get the word to the Moon, she screamed again. '*Gilll!*'

Agnes tossed the match. The grain on the floor ignited with a *whoosh!* Prairie screamed.

○　○　○

23

Oblivion

Agnes ran towards the ladder. Over the thrum of the flames Prairie heard the door above the ladder open.

'*Prairie?*' Olive's voice.

'*Prairie?*' That was Constable Timms. Did she imagine it?

'*Down here. Please help me!*' Prairie screamed. She coughed, choking. Smoke was filling the room. 'Be careful!' she croaked. 'Agnes is down here!'

Emmanuel Timms pulled his revolver out and aimed blindly into the smoke-filled pit.

'Stay where you are, Agnes Comfrey,' he said. 'I won't think twice about shooting you.'

Agnes turned from the ladder and ran towards the grain elevator, scaling the internal mechanism through the rising smoke haze.

'She's getting away,' yelled Prairie.

'*Prairie!*' Olive's voice was shrill, 'Can you climb the ladder?'

'My hands and feet are tied!'

'I'm coming down!' That was Timms. The jerrycan ignited with a bang, and Olive screamed.

A thought hit Prairie like a lightning bolt. Her father's voice again. She had to help herself. She couldn't risk the life of Emmanuel Timms as well as her own.

Come on, Prairie girl.

She did this all the time in physical education at school. Could she still do it? She flopped onto her left side, tucked herself into a ball, as small as she could make herself, and then slid her hands under her backside and over her feet. The bindings on her wrists caught on her heels. She screamed at the pain.

Timms was racing backwards down the ladder. He was soon with her and pulled her to her feet. There wasn't time to untie the knots of her fastenings. He half-dragged, half-carried her to the ladder and pushed her clumsily up it. When she got close enough to the top, Olive heaved her into the storeroom, tumbling backwards with the effort. Another explosion rocked the room below.

'We need to get out now,' Timms choked with the effort of climbing up after Prairie. The smoke was acrid and suffocating. In the undignified manner of a potato sack, he hoisted Prairie over his shoulder, and he and Olive fled the storeroom, coughing and gasping for fresh air. When he judged they were far enough away, he set Prairie down on the gravel of the haul road, as gently as his own failing strength would permit.

Tears streamed in white rivers down Prairie's soot-stained face. Olive cradled her and smoothed her hair, saying, 'We'll get you some water as soon as I untie these fucking things.' She went to work on the knots at Prairie's wrists.

A flash in the window of the grain elevator drew Prairie's eye.

'Look,' she croaked weakly.

'Good God,' murmured Timms, as he and Olive turned to follow her gaze.

There, near the very top of the silo, leaning out of the grain elevator's uppermost window, was Agnes Comfrey. Smoke billowed below her. As they watched, aghast, Agnes climbed out of the window and onto the sloping roof.

'Good God,' said Timms again. 'She's going to jump.'

'Good riddance,' Olive spat through gritted teeth. Prairie's throat was too raw to give voice to her thoughts.

Death, for Agnes, seemed unavoidable. But to jump or to be burned alive? Either was a terrible choice. Prairie hoped that in death, Agnes would find a freedom she'd never managed in life. She closed her eyes and sent a silent prayer to the top of the silo.

Agnes Comfrey looked at the sky and held her arms aloft. The smoke billowed below, and the flames roared and popped. They would engulf her soon. Would she asphyxiate first? She looked out across the black fields of Wheatsheaf and smiled, thinking of her father.

'Soon, Father,' she said. 'I will see you.' Then she thought of her mother and her smile faded. Would she be there too? She would be angry with Agnes for the wicked thing she had done. There would be no forgiveness for Agnes Comfrey. Only endless torment for her spirit.

I hope there is no Heaven or Hell, Agnes thought. *I hope there is just oblivion.*

'Don't look!' Timms turned swiftly and used his body to shield the women from the sight of the tormented woman plummeting the equivalent of ten storeys to the hard-packed earth below. They heard the impact. Prairie groaned.

'Don't look,' said Timms again. Gently, he helped Olive lift Prairie and between them, with their backs to the broken body of Agnes Comfrey, they took Prairie to the waiting patrol car.

Epilogue

Throughout the Winter, the fields lay fallow and accepted the rain with gratitude. The exchange hummed and blinked and connected the townsfolk, who for weeks could talk about nothing but the fire.

'A cornucopia of snakes,' said Prunella Battersby to Irma Vickery, describing the Comfrey homestead. 'As the mother, so is the daughter.'

'Ooh, I know!' said Irma Vickery, thinking about how much she hated Prunella Battersby.

'That Mister Sanders from Blush Salt is so handsome,' said Felice Banbury to Joyce Early. 'Didn't I always say it wasn't him?'

'You said you *always* thought it was him, Felice,' said Joyce. 'You owe me five dollars.'

Olive Wellshorn demanded that Fidel Peterson reinstate Mabel Wattage – *with* apology. What Olive said to Peterson was never clear, but he complied with her request and never another word was said about it.

Olive thought about the day of the fire a lot. As they'd raced to the silo in the patrol car, Olive, clutching the doorhandle to keep from screaming, had looked across at Timms and asked, *'How do you know Agnes has taken Prairie there?'*

Timms had shrugged, his eyes firmly fixed on the road. *'I don't,'* he'd replied grimly. *'But on the kitchen table there was a picture of Agnes Comfrey with her father, surrounded by a field of wheat. I recognised the silos in the background. They feature quite a bit in our tale, Miss Wellshorn. Too often for coincidence, I pray.'*

Days after the fire, Jim Reynolds' tow-truck pulled a blue Morris Minor and a red Mini out of the dam in the soot-blackened shadow of the burned-out silo. He and Eli Schwartz quietly set about putting the blue car to rights and before Winter's end, they presented it, pristine and shining, to Prairie Humble, who wept with gratitude.

At the beginning of September, Emmanuel Timms sat his Senior Constable's exam in Golga. He passed with flying colours and was offered a post in the far Western cereal fields. He chose to remain a constable, at his desk in his red brick station at the end of Grain Street. The people of Wheatsheaf needed him. And he needed them.

As the Sun of the Vernal Equinox dipped her belly in the mirror-glass of Blush Lake, Gil and Prairie watched her bathe.

'The company is sending me to Esperance for a bit,' said Gil unhappily.

'Don't look so glum' said Prairie, smiling. 'I'm sure they have an exchange or two in the West.' She added slyly, 'You know how to use a phone, after all.' She put her head on his shoulder, and they laughed.

O O O

And throughout the Spring, the vast fields of wheat grew and turned golden in the sun of Summer. And their ears listened to all the words uttered and brought to them on the warm winds. They listened carefully. For words matter.

Fine